COMATOSE

A NOVEL BY

MATTHEW ROBERTS

Cover Art by Matthew Roberts, Hannah Roberts
Edited by: *The Big Three:* Micah Summers, Sandy Roberts, and Carissa Arend, without whom the story might still be languishing in development hell.

ISBN 978-1-365-04101-3

First Printing: 2016

CONTENTS

To

Mrs. Shields,
Who woke me when I was *Comatose*.

Awaken, soul
By moon's soft glow
And let thy senses overflow
For didst thee wake this eve to find
Something departed, yet escapes thy mind?

No, said I, it cannot be,
The one I love is lost to me,
Search my soul, search and recall,
The one we never knew at all.

See, my soul, that empty bed,
Whereon our love would lay her head,
Now 'tis filled with vacant dreams,
Specters prowl within the seams.

We sank into those haunted skies
But saw no love, despite our tries,
And in our search the secrets grew,
threatened to strangle all we knew.

Search, my soul, on these stormy seas,
And shout—My love, we call to thee!
Then cringe away from titanic waves
Revealing sleepers in sunken graves.

Watch them drowse beneath the brine,
Dreaming of lands they left behind,
While we, the living, have yet to dwell,
On worlds that we have lost to Hell.

Until that moment, when we unite,
Against ignorance and despair I fight,
And resist the calls of the mentally dead,
Who have chosen worlds of fiction instead.

ONE

"Unbelievable."

"Ah, but we expected it, didn't we?"

"No, sir—"

"Hand me the police report, Ms. McPherson."

"Of course, sir."

"Nine bodies were found in the building, Ms. McPherson. The police concluded that the cause of death was starvation. Remembering, surely, that the deceased were trapped in a tavern stocked with food, and for merely two days, at that?"

"This is why the investigations fall to us, sir."

"Mayor Kaufmann usually doesn't trust us. Surely our reputation, by now, has convinced him otherwise?"

"He is out of his league, Mr. Powers."

"Ah, Demetria. Kaufmann is a wise man; he knows when a police investigation is sufficient and when one is not. Even he realizes that murder is a crime for the Academy to solve, and none other."

"Murder, sir?"

"One would be blind not to see it. Take a team with you, Ms. McPherson. Throw around some 'supernatural,' if it's appropriate. From these initial reports, one without a grounding in the sciences would be quick to blame the incident on paranormal activities, don't you agree?"

"Certainly—but why contribute to the hysteria?"

"I've heard it makes Kaufmann uncomfortable. And he should be. Ah, we all should be."

I.

NOW IT CAME TO PASS, LATE UPON A RATHER WINDBLOWN FRIDAY evening, a blizzard of ferocious strength settled upon the City of Comatose. The howling wind stampeded through the streets, stripping the trees of their leaves like a crazed barber. The clouds blanketed the buildings with soft deposits of snow—and sharp spears of ice.

Comatose, less than twelve blocks long from end to end, could hardly call itself a "city" on account of its size. Despite this, the settlement was governed under a mayor and an elected council. Due to its remote location, it grew its own food and operated in extreme isolation.

In that respect, it could call itself whatever it wished.

Avenues Grande and Morpheus intersected each other by means of a traffic circle at the city's center, forming a well-travelled neighborhood called the Cross. On the extremities of Avenue Grande were the two most important establishments of the village —the city hall, and a huge, sprawling university known as the Academy. It was this university that placed Comatose on the map— it anchored them against the twilight obscurity that threatened to swallow the town.

The main building of the Academy was a sharpened glass skyscraper, a monument of poise and contemporary elegance. Its layered design and towering spires gave it the appearance of a crystalline flower, just opening its petals to the brisk dawn. At the ground level, triangular glass sculptures encircled the structure and cast the entryway in a splendid aquamarine hue.

In absolute contrast, the derelict city hall operated out of a remodeled warehouse.

On the first morning since the blizzard's recession, the clouds lingered in the sky, as if in deliberation about the necessity of further inclement weather. The storm's deferral occasioned a gloomy, dismal atmosphere for the City of Comatose. Snow, still lightly falling, painted the entire city like a newspaper: utterly colorless, absent of vibrancy. There, in the wake of the storm, in the tallowed floors of an unsavory tavern, the phenomenon was discovered.

They made no noise as they glided—like ghosts—across the sprawling main road.

A caravan of sleek, white, luxury cars, dispatched from the Academy.

Silently, the phantoms traversed the empty, snow-covered streets of Comatose, perhaps boasting their early advantage over the sleeping citizens. The phantoms were *alive*—the citizens were yet to awaken.

Swiftly, this caravan—this fleet of ghostly coaches—reached their destination: *The Charming Highwayman*, a tavern of questionable repute. The vehicles lined up neatly beside the pub. Passengers disembarked. Men and women retrieved their polished white briefcases and nimbly crossed under the yellow police tape which now surrounded the perimeter of the building.

From the foremost car, a chauffeur of visible stateliness stepped out, walked around the front of the vehicle, and opened the rear passenger door. An older woman dressed in snow-white business apparel was sitting inside, typing some quick notes on her laptop. She neither glanced at nor paid attention to the driver, but wordlessly closed her computer and stepped out into the crisp morning air.

The woman briskly strode past the police barrier and allowed her piercing, pale green eyes to examine every minute detail that the snow attempted to conceal. Behind her, the driver sauntered over, holding a phone before him.

"I have Mayor Kaufmann on the line, Ma'am."

"Does he have information?"

The chauffeur paused and delivered a brief glance of annoyance, but relayed the question to the mayor.

"He says that he would rather pose that question to you, as you happen to be—"

"You may tell Kaufmann that the Academy runs its investigations on a strict policy of confidentiality, and that he may inquire at Mr. Powers' office when the report has been completed."

The woman in the white business apparel turned around pointedly and entered the building.

The chauffeur frowned, but he politely altered her words as he answered the mayor. "Ms. McPherson is beginning the investigation as we speak, sir. She says you may retrieve a summary at Mr. Powers' office this evening."

Inside, the white-clad investigators had already created a laboratory of sorts. Briefcases opened, transforming into collapsible tables with beakers and flasks full of complex chemical solutions. Other briefcases contained computers, cameras, and other fantastic devices that would allow their analysis swift and effortless completion.

Ms. McPherson surveyed the room slowly. She allowed her piercing, pale green eyes to examine every minute detail that the dust attempted to conceal. The investigators behind her began recording the scene of the crime with their panoramic cameras. Their data would prove invaluable in recreating the crime scene when they returned to the Academy.

Nine bodies were located in various places about the room, but Ms. McPherson immediately decided that none of them looked very dead. Some of the bodies were seated at tables, others were found leaning against the wall...a pair of young men in the far corner seemed frozen in mid-laughter.

Something was wrong. She was not accustomed to this "worried" feeling. She had been in this field too long for that.

"Get me a blood sample, immediately," she ordered.

"Ma'am? We haven't even completed—"

"Do it!"

An investigator who was standing by the largest chemical table unwrapped a sterile hypodermic needle and moved to the nearest body. It was a young male, a smile still on his bearded face, a fork still in his dead grasp.

The man with the syringe placed his hand on the front of the neck as he prepared to draw blood from the artery within. And suddenly the investigator bounded back from the corpse as if he had been struck.

"Hell!" he shrieked. The syringe clattered to the floor.

Ms. McPherson spun around with a sharp, questioning glare.

"The body..." the man gasped, "It still has a pulse!"

Two

"All nine had a pulse?"

"Yes, sir. I tried to have the bodies taken to Forensics, but Pruitt wouldn't let me."

"It was good of him to stop you, and foolish of you to try."

"Sir, you surely understand how crucial the bodies are to the investigations."

"You and I both know that the bodies would have been studied at the morgue, which is no place for the living."

"We haven't concluded that they are still alive, sir."

"Don't be ridiculous, Demetria. You have the blood samples and the rest of the data, I presume?"

"No, sir. Pruitt said that it was unethical to collect the necessary data from living people without their consent."

"Perhaps that move was too conservative."

"It was completely disruptive to our work."

"We are unaccustomed to dealing with murders that do not involve absolute death. Until this morning I had not even heard of such a concept. But in our business, caution is invaluable. Mr. Pruitt did the right thing."

"Sir? How is my team to study the bodies now that they have been moved to the hospital? We have no custody over them."

"You must call Mayor Kaufmann and have him dispatch a police officer to facilitate the examination. And I will notify Harrison and tell him to ease off."

"Of course. And sir?"

"Yes, Demetria."

"Do you still believe this was murder?"

"Oh yes. But murder of a different sort."

I.

THE MAYORAL DEPARTMENT OF THE CITY OF COMATOSE WAS ENCLOSED in a second story loft overlooking the vast warehouse that housed the municipal headquarters. Downstairs, an occasional secretary might pass by on their way from one department to another, but the wide expanses of the building saw little use save for the storage of old documents. It was generally understood by the entire staff that if those documents had instead been thrown to the shredder, no real harm would come from it.

So sparse were the filled positions that the various members of the administration could station their cubicles in odd corners or niches between the towering shelves, and by means of an office-wide intranet, feasibly complete all their work without encountering another human being.

In his office above the warehouse, a certain Mr. Samuel Kaufmann, the elected leader of the town, worked a thankless and unforgiving job.

Tall and awkward, Kaufmann was plagued with a variety of discomforts—in particular, an incessant difficulty when it came to purchasing suits. The sleeves would generally be too short, and if not, then the breadth would most assuredly be too wide. The town had no tailor—that was a job for the machines. Adding to his rather sloppy appearance was the inadequate growth of his facial hair. Though Kaufmann shaved piously, the whiskers and stubble would stubbornly return before noon, and then cease to grow any further. Providence, it seemed, had simply fated him with the curse of unattractiveness.

Consistent with this description, Kaufmann was not a very respected man. One might venture that though his intentions were noble, they were marred by an exceptionally slow execution. Surely, not his fault. The damnable councilmembers, the damnable Academy...what an awful city he had to contend with. The virtues he had naïvely brought into his office had been destroyed by bureaucracy and corruption. Perhaps he had misunderstood the power that came along with being Mayor? It seemed now that the city council kept him on only to offer a destination for complaints and petitions—and blame, should any of their backroom deals go awry.

"I didn't want this reelection, Miss Brady," he grumbled to the secretary, a quiet woman with deep orange hair. "I should've called it quits and let the other candidates sort it out."

"As I recall, Mr. Kaufmann," she replied, "you were the only candidate."

Kaufmann chuckled morosely. "So I was. This city's gone to the dogs."

"You intend to fix that, sir?"

"Fix it? Hell," he muttered, "when the councilors get off their blessed backsides, maybe *then* we'll see some fixing!"

But here he sat, behind the brass plaque that read *Mayor Samuel Kaufmann*. Here he sat amongst the empty desks of the understaffed, underfunded city hall...in the city where no one wanted to be mayor...

The phone rang. He stirred. It was typical of Miss Brady to handle the calls, but the phone on his desk possessed a number different from the public listing. Calls that came directly to him were, therefore, of greater importance.

"Mayor Kaufmann on the line," he said, a little too excitedly.

"This is Demetria McPherson, Forensics Chair at the Academy," a placid voice replied.

So he was to be graced by the cordiality of the Academy, then! How thoughtful of them to deliver the findings after all!

"I thought I'd have to request the results," he said coolly.

"You still do."

These damnable snobs from the Academy.

"A little respect would suit you well," he said, almost a complaint.

"I'm calling to request the presence of a police officer to accompany my team as we examine the victims at the hospital."

He was not aware of any survivors. Once again he had been subjected to the shroud—if a piece of knowledge did not serve as a convenience to the knower, it was not disclosed at all. But the semblance of professionalism was key here: he'd have to lie.

Of course he knew about the victims.

"Yes, I'll have an officer meet your team there," he replied, his voice rising in pace with how *finished* he was with this blasted conversation.

"You will instruct him to stay out of our way," Ms. McPherson continued, "It is difficult enough to run these evaluations without simpletons such as yourself butting into the process."

Kaufmann did not expect the insult, but like anyone would, he did not allow it to stand.

"Now see here! I am to be treated with the respect I am due, or so help me I will terminate municipal funding to your organization!"

The threat, of course, was empty.

"Enjoy your evening, Mr. Kaufmann," she said, the cruel smile transmitting across the wire, the click of the dropped line ending their adverse conversation.

Kaufmann dropped a fat, juicy expletive. He let his fingers rise toward his aching temples, and as he massaged them, his gaze drifted to the secretary. Though customary of him to ignore her, he suddenly paid attention to this woman and her bright amber hair. He suddenly noticed her delicate fingers clacking at the keys of the ancient, cut-rate computer. He suddenly contemplated the woman who was neither his friend nor his enemy, the woman whose first name was still unknown to him, the woman who was but a stranger in a world of strangeness...

Seeking another source for information, he dialed a new number.

"Yes, I'd like to speak with Mr. Powers, please. No, I would not like to hold, it's rather important. No—hey! This is the Mayor of Comatose on the line—"

He set the phone down again. He cradled his face in his hands, quite fed up with the undue disrespect he'd endured today. What was the point of having a mayor if the leadership position never received its due regard? What was the point of having a mayor if his authority was merely acknowledged subjectively?

Another call came in, but it was destined to be ignored. If these ungrateful citizens called only to belittle his political sacrifice, then he would not suffer himself endure it any more. He was through! *Find better things to do!* he screamed at the invisible identity of the waiting caller.

"Sir, your phone is ringing. Are you going to answer it?" Miss Brady called.

"I shall never speak with a human again, Miss Brady, that is *your* job!" he retorted, exaggerating his plight as if it were comparable to crucifixion.

She nodded in amusement and answered the call: "You've reached the Office of the Mayor, may I help you?"

She nodded again, and cast a wary glance to Kaufmann. "It's for you," she mouthed.

"I am currently conferencing with an important diplomat from Peru," Kaufmann mouthed back.

Miss Brady shook her head in skeptical uncertainty. The useless secretary did not understand his silent words!

"It's Morgan Powers, weren't you trying to reach—"

"You could've said that the first time!" he exclaimed, picking up his receiver.

"Kaufmann speaking," he grumbled.

"Mr. Mayor? This is Morgan Powers from the Academy. I heard you were trying to reach me."

Kaufmann perked up. "I was."

"I must apologize for the poor treatment you received on the phone. I assure you that it will not happen again."

"This is not the first time, Mr. Powers. A certain Ms. McPherson was also very brisk with me this afternoon," Kaufmann added.

"I will see that it is dealt with," the man said politely.

"I wanted to inquire about the investigations this morning. Is there any news?"

"A little. The bodies discovered in the tavern are not quite dead, but instead appear to be in a prolonged state of unconsciousness."

"A coma, sir?"

"It's interesting that you say that, Mr. Mayor. Do you know what 'coma' is short for?"

Kaufmann almost replied, but something held him back. It surprised him that he had not immediately made the connection.

"Comatose. The...the name of our city," he whispered. Somewhat subdued, Kaufmann ventured no more words—and apparently weary of waiting, Mr. Powers moved to terminate the call.

"I bid you a good evening, Mr. Mayor."

Kaufmann set the phone down a third time.

"How late will you be in tonight, Miss Brady?"

She looked at him with a degree of exhaustion. "About 11:30. If these invoices don't get to the council by tomorrow, they're going to have a fit. I could run and grab some burgers and add them to the bill?"

Kaufmann smiled. "Clock O.T. and make it a meal."

II.

HOURS PASSED WITHOUT VERBAL EXCHANGE BETWEEN THE MAYOR AND his secretary. Kaufmann made calls through the evening, but eventually the businesses and agencies closed for the night. Soon, the only lights in town (save for the splendor of the Academy's campus) gleamed from the City Hall. During this ungodly hour, Kaufmann sunk lower and lower toward his desk, until his head rested on his crossed arms and his hand idly scratched words onto a memorandum. The pen dropped—he drifted away quietly.

III.

AND THEN, HIS EYES FLUTTERED OPEN.

Ha! He'd fallen asleep at his desk!

He would not be troubled to raise his head at such a moment, but holding to the assumption that the secretary was in much better command of her wakefulness than he at his, Kaufmann mumbled into his arm: "What time is it, Miss Brady?"

He lay there for a few more seconds, but eventually he sat up.

Miss Brady was seated in front of his desk, staring at him.

"Goddammit!" Kaufmann bellowed, scooting away. "What the devil's gotten into you?"

She did not answer him, not with words, at least. Her wide, hazel eyes displayed a deep, vacant interest in the boundless, empty space in front of her. Her amber locks framed a pale, inanimate face.

"...Miss Brady?"

The woman whose first name he did not know.

There was a small slip of paper on the desk, between them. He lifted it to meet his eyes:

Her name was Amelia.

Dropping the note in shock, Kaufmann met her unmoving eyes once more and glanced at her arm. A deft movement brought her wrist to his desk, where he placed a thumb over the artery.

He found a pulse.

But somehow, he knew that she was dead.

THREE

"This was murder."

"I can almost agree with you now, sir. But...she's still alive, just like the rest."

"They will never wake up again, Ms. McPherson. Never! What is life without the brain? It's not life at all; it's merely existence. That, I say, is death."

"Very well, sir."

"What did the analysis of the first nine reveal?"

"Nothing factual. No fingerprints left behind, no signs of struggle, not even the prick one would expect from a needle. We can only speculate."

"And of the secretary?"

"Again, nothing on the body. Your 'murderer,' however, left some key evidence behind."

"What kind of evidence? Careless...or intentional?"

"Intentional, sir."

"Tell me."

"The note was typed, no fingerprints. It read, Her name was Amelia."

"Just like David and Saul in the cave."

"Sir?"

"An old Bible tale. King Saul enters a cave to rest, not knowing that his God-guided enemy is hiding deeper within. When Saul emerges, David calls to him, displaying a piece of fabric that he cut from Saul's robe."

"And?"

"It means, Ms. McPherson, that David could have killed the king in the darkness of the cave, but instead chose to flaunt his

power. Indeed, our murderer could have
taken the life of the Mayor. So why did he
hold back?"

I.

IN A SMALL OFFICE ON THE CORNER OF THE MAIN INTERSECTION THAT
comprised Comatose, there worked a young woman by the name of
Melissa McCain. She was the daughter of a respected and reputable
detective known throughout the forensic field as Jarvis McCain.
Jarvis had worked for the Academy in his glory days, but now lived
a quiet, retired life on his ranch in the forested hills above
Comatose.

Melissa had followed his footsteps in becoming an
investigator, but she had no wish to work for an established
company. With a contribution from her father, who had taken a
philanthropic interest in her career, Melissa opened a private
investigative firm in the heart of the city. From her desk she could
clearly see the iconic traffic circle of the Cross, obscured only by the
frosted window lettering that read PARAGON PRIVATE
INVESTIGATIONS.

Morning had arrived, and as Melissa began to ask herself
whether the desk *really* needed cleaning, she glimpsed a lone figure
crossing the street, battling against crisp gusts of wind and
sprinkling snow. Her eyes drifted down toward her desk, to a
recently closed case concerning a love affair, a bar fight, and
ultimately the arrest of every client involved in the mystery.
Paragon's sleuthing revealed, among other things, that their
services were engaged by a chronic bankrupt.

The door flew open; the silent office filled itself with
screaming wind and the jingle of sleigh bells tied to the door. A tall
stranger stood at the threshold, holding the door open as if to let in
as much snow as possible, unaware of the nuisance his inaction
caused.

Melissa glared. The stranger blinked, stumbled deeper into
the building, and used his foot to kick the door closed. It bounced
open, and he tried again, and by now Melissa had begun to wonder

if her lot in life solely revolved around working for such pitiful riffraff.

Somewhere in her mind, two neurons compared notes, and realized that this stranger was quite recognizable.

It was the Mayor of Comatose.

And suddenly, he was her client.

"I assume you are Miss McCain?" the man murmured. He tossed his coat on a hatstand, caused it to topple, and imagined a stream of charming (and very unspoken) apologies to venture as he stooped to retrieve it.

"Yes, Mr. Mayor. At your service, as always," she said, holding back surprise. She was quite adept at this kind of concealment—it was the culminating result borne from years of practice. With an abrupt cessation of body language and a forceful shift of emotion, she directed her feelings elsewhere and left her mind to face situations unhindered by sentiment.

"Oh. why...well, I appreciate that, Miss McCain," the Mayor replied, jumping across the sentence as one jumps across a stream wearing nice shoes. "Your father—nice guy, Jarvis—he referred you to me—I mean…"

Melissa nodded, understanding. The Mayor was not an infrequent topic to be heard from her father's lips.

"Samuel Kaufmann," her father once said, *"the only man foolish enough to run for political office in a town that wants no leader, no government, and no trouble."*

Like the unpopular family member who tries to evoke conversation out of the strangled throes of silence...

"He's spoken of you several times," she replied, obscuring all negativity behind a shroud of half-truth.

"I trust your father on this matter, and, well, he agrees with my...er, my decision. You've heard news—oh, but surely you have?"

"I'm a detective Mr. Kaufmann, not a mind-reader," Melissa chided mildly.

His head boggled in frustration at his inability to express himself. "Why, the deaths that occurred at *The Charming Highwayman*, of course!"

Behind a featureless countenance, her mind erupted with confusion. Had such a remarkable event escaped her?

"No, sir."

The man looked at her peculiarly. Comatose was a small town, but for some reason news did not circulate very quickly here. Information was cold syrup flowing from a freshly thawed container. Here, in this city, the only 'news' one needed was confined to the borders of one's own house:

Ah! Here's the daily update on the lawn height. And there's the statistical analysis on the tarnishing of the silverware!

"No matter," the man called, snapping out of his stupor. "Nine bodies were discovered in the tavern, but it was realized that all of them were still alive, in what we believe to be permanent comas."

Melissa displayed no surprise—her adept concealment—but she still internalized her questions. She wondered if the strange deaths were more surprising than the fact that she hadn't heard the news before.

"I assume the Academy has evaluated the initial scene of the crime?"

"Yes, yes. But something far worse has happened."

Melissa said nothing, prompting Kaufmann to continue.

"My secretary, Miss McCain!" This time, Melissa's emotional suppression failed her. The Mayor's voice erupted with volume, his awkward and unintentionally destructive personage was now pacing the room, endangering it. "We were in the same building at the same time and someone killed her when he could have killed me! My nerves are bleeding more that she did!"

"Was she close to you?" Melissa asked.

"Close to me? Maybe by a desk or two. But *close* to me? Dammit, I didn't even know her first name before this absurd tragedy!"

Melissa was suddenly afraid of this man and the dangerous case that he brought here. But she could not say no so quickly. Not to a man who was just as afraid as she was.

She raised a hand to comb through her hair, then cursed the nervous habit and directed the hand instead to a shelf behind her, grasping something she knew would not be there. "Has the Academy rejected the job?"

"No, they're investigating too. They're snaking all over the place, slithering into my privacy and poisoning my career! And I can't rely on them, Miss McCain, I can't be dependent on people like that. I need facts, Miss McCain, I need 'em straight and true."

"I'll take the case," Melissa said firmly, "but I need to know how you expect the Academy to coexist with us."

"In all honesty," he replied, his eyes displaying a rare twinkle of humor, "I don't know if cooperation will ever exist between you and them. And that's primarily their fault."

"If they expel us from the crime scene or withhold any evidence, I can't say we'll be able to do much good."

"Oh, that won't be a problem. The Academy is a private investigation service like yourself, paid for by the city...ah, shall we say for lack of a competent police force? As long as I'm Mayor, they can't keep you from the job."

She looked up at the clock. There was still time to take a look at the Mayor's office, where his secretary had met her demise.

"I'll take the case," she repeated. "Any other instructions?"

The mayor gathered his coat, making sure, this time, to keep the hatstand steady. "You are to report to me every evening with any news you find." He was enjoying this position of true authority. "Since the Academy has refused to deliver information this way, I will have to request it—perhaps I can compare yours and theirs...find the discrepancies..."

He stepped toward the door, and then looked back with a bewildered countenance. "I suppose, well, we're, ah...done here? I mean, unless there is something else to be arranged?"

"My associates and I will meet with you after our initial observation to confirm our interest in the case," Melissa replied, grabbing at the chance to secure an escape clause.

"Right." He looked at her questioningly, and then confirmed to himself his intention to depart. "Right, right." He stepped outside and began the long trek whence he came. The curling wind, which had picked up slightly that morning, shuffled some snow into the warm office as the door closed.

Melissa watched the tall, skeletal man dissipate into the fog —and wondered if the world she knew would eventually do the same.

Four

"Kaufmann has done something most unexpectedly foolish."

"Hm? I was unaware that he could be more senseless than we already know him to be."

"I would not encourage such an attitude so early in the game, Ms. McPherson."

"My apologies, sir."

"Kaufmann has informed me that we are to share all evidence and reports with a private investigative firm known as Paragon PI. The existence of a competent investigator outside of the Academy astounds me."

"There are no competent investigators outside of the Academy."

"A conclusion you seem to have reached without evidence."

"Very well, sir. I'm researching the organization as we speak."

"And?"

"The company is run by Melissa McC—"

"Jarvis?"

"...His daughter, sir."

"Kaufmann has placed his trust in a more capable individual than I thought..."

"We will not let them snatch the success that belongs to us."

"I am more concerned that Kaufmann has finally decided to extend his independence beyond that which has been handed to him. He is no longer solely dependent on us."

"Is that a bad thing, sir?"

"We at the Academy are very careful to keep our hands clean and our children safe. I can no longer insulate Kaufmann nor his friends at Paragon. They are going to get themselves killed."

"As the old saying goes, sir, 'Curiosity killed the—'"

"I would prefer, Ms. McPherson, to avoid hearing such clichés."

I.

CALVIN BARKER, FROM A CROUCHING POSITION ON THE FLOOR OF THE mayoral department, glanced up from the carpet. "Yes, Myles, it *is* a spot. Whether it's *blood* is another matter entirely."

"There can be no other explanation because it's obviously blood!" the other replied, his voice boasting a broad, golden tone.

Calvin almost sighed, but an ever-present compulsion to correct his associate prompted a response instead. "Myles, we already know that the victim suffered no lacerations or punctures of any kind!"

"That's not what I meant," he replied with a clever smile. His eyes twinkled with a complacent assurance of his own accuracy. "The blood must therefore be the *murderer's*. I read this book once where a villain named Bloody Bradley goes and confuses everybody by—"

"Furthermore," Calvin cried, rising to his feet, "We have already been assured by the Academy that they have performed Luminol tests on the stain and came to the conclusion that *no blood was found anywhere in the room.* Satisfied?"

"Well, that's a *possible* explanation," Myles conceded, squirming his way out of a now obvious mistake. "The murderer's clearly too smart for the both of us."

Calvin blinked. "No, Myles. It is *the* explanation. You've just wasted two minutes of our time, looking for evidence to validate your half-baked imagination."

A woman's voice called across the room. "We're all making wrong assumptions until we find the killer, Calvin."

He rose, casting an annoyed look in his coworker's direction. She was carefully examining a desk in the far corner of the mayoral department, where they had worked for the past hour now, alongside a team of investigators from the Academy.

"Melissa, what do you really intend to find over there?" he called. "She died next to Kaufmann's desk, not over there."

Calvin was the logical one on his team. Though praised for his quick deduction and his intricate, almost immediate understanding of any situation, Calvin was not a creative thinker. When logic failed him...things went to Melissa.

"What makes you think that?"

"Why, because that's where—"

His cheek twitched in sudden comprehension. "I mean, that's where we found the body." He smiled sheepishly. "But that's nothing, isn't it?"

"Yeah." She returned the grin.

The voice of the Academy's lead investigator broke in: "I would not be so quick to write off your companion's supposition, Miss McCain."

Calvin turned toward the speaker with surprise. Ms. McPherson, as he had so far encountered her, was not a woman given to acknowledging other people's contributions—unless the contributions were in fact setbacks. *Then* the scorn would flow freely.

McPherson stepped closer. "Our overwhelming suspicion is that Miss Brady met her untimely end while in front of Mr. Kaufmann's desk—where they were likely conferring together," she continued.

Melissa shot a withering stare at the woman—the suggestion was ridiculous! "Whatever in your research lead you to draw that conclusion?"

Melissa's gaze was returned with frigid hostility. "It follows as the most logical explanation," McPherson replied.

"It most certainly does not!" Melissa retorted. "But considering you've had almost no communication with the closest man we have to a witness, Mr. Kaufmann, I can almost see how you might faultily assume that. Kaufmann has informed me that he was aware of Miss Brady's presence at her own desk—up to the point when he fell asleep. Might you explain to us, Ms. McPherson, the profit in a conference between a young secretary and her sleeping employer?"

The woman only scowled in reply.

Calvin watched the feud in disappointment. Melissa held sentiments of extreme opposition toward working with the Academy and its people, never missing an opportunity to patronize and disparage her chief competitors in the investigative industry. Calvin might've ignored her behavior, had it not been for their similar responses. From the outside, he knew the two groups must look like factions of arguing teenagers.

Melissa's expression suddenly changed. Calvin, who had been idly watching her, noted that one of her hands was fingering the underside of the desk she stood by.

When Melissa spoke again, her voice had changed as well. "I would also ask of you to account for the writing I've just discovered under the secretary's desk."

The room seemed to explode in activity! A bland, translucent layer of apathy was suddenly washed away in a torrential influx of excitement as Melissa's victorious discovery unfolded. Calvin and Myles brightened and forgot their quarrel, while McPherson's lined and wrinkled face grew tauter with another feeling she was unaccustomed to in the forensics field— panic.

"Step away from there, Miss McCain!" the woman barked. Melissa shook her head, reveling in her newfound control over the situation and laughing internally at McPherson's hope to steal that glory from her.

"Calvin, come over and bring a notepad," Melissa called, procuring a flashlight from her supplies and lying on her back so as to observe her discovery. Calvin knelt next to her with a pen in hand, and wrote down letters as she decoded the unruly scrawls.

"From the shakiness of the handwriting, I would speculate that this message was written close to the time of death," Melissa murmured, "not to mention in other circumstances, she would've used a different medium to create her note."

"Miss McCain—"

"I need silence, Ms. McPherson," Melissa snapped. To her coworker, she whispered: "Here's another 'Y,' Calvin."

"A second one?"

"Spelling error, probably—and it's getting more unruly, which could indicate an increase in haste—even desperation!" She paused, then hummed in a low voice as she deciphered the subsequent characters. "'E,' that one's obvious. And the last one's a 'D.'" She stood up, and Calvin set the notepad on the desk for all to see.

"It reads: *'THEYVE BETRAYYED'*," Calvin announced. "'*They've Betrayed...*' what? Who?"

There was silence in the room as the investigators pondered the meaning behind the cryptic clue. Melissa, meanwhile, had interested herself in something else. She ran her index finger over the surface of the desk, smelled whatever she had picked up, and then tasted it.

"There are traces of sweat here, too," she murmured.

"It all fits together, Melissa!" Myles cried in triumph. "If *I* were faced with a murderer, I'd be sweating all over the place!"

Most everyone in the room shot him a withering stare, but Myles did not notice. Presently he had begun to pace around the room importantly, idly flicking ashes from his cigar onto the carpet and smirking at his wittiness.

"Check Kaufmann's desk," she ordered. Calvin obliged and rapidly confirmed her suspicion—there was no trace of the substance there.

Melissa turned to the members of the room again. Her excitement was building.

"The secretary must've been killed before she was moved to Kaufmann's workspace."

"We at the Academy are always—"

"Spare me. What information do you have regarding the note you found on Kaufmann's desk?"

"It's typed, Miss McCain, I'm sure you've noticed—"

"I did," Myles announced.

"...It's printed on standard, 0.25 millimeter card stock, no fingerprints—"

"Stats, stats. They're useful, until they suddenly *aren't*," Melissa interrupted. "Did you read between the lines, beyond simply the *content* of the note?"

"Since you seem to have, Miss McCain, please, enlighten us," Ms. McPherson replied, austere and frosty.

"Again, your lack of communication with Mr. Kaufmann is a startling disadvantage. I have spoken with him, and he has very firmly told me that he never even knew the first name of his secretary."

"And?"

"The note. It reads, '*Her name was Amelia*'."

"Which helps us...how?"

"It gives us insight into this killer's intentions. This was not a threat to him personally, but a taunt—and definitely intended to psychologically destabilize him."

Calvin glanced at the ground, but Melissa kept talking.

"We can also infer that the murderer is quite familiar with Kaufmann—how else would this killer have any knowledge about Kaufmann's relationship to his secretary? How would the killer know whether Kaufmann *knew* her name? How would—"

"Yes, of course, Miss McCain," Ms. Mcpherson interjected, in a tone drastically different from the bored persona she had previously portrayed. Calvin found himself suddenly intrigued by the woman's new attitude.

"My! Are these yours, Miss McCain?" she cried, walking toward a small fold-up TV table which bore several chemical arrangements and other glassware.

"They belong to my team, yes."

McPherson took hold of a flask, examined it with a total lack of enthusiasm, and set it down at the far edge of the table. In doing so, she caused the entire structure to cave in and collapse. The glassware, with a deafening clamor, shattered on the floor and stained it in multifarious hues.

"Oh, dear! I'm dreadfully sorry. I'm always *such* a klutz, especially around other people's belongings."

Melissa and Calvin, appalled by the destruction and unimpressed by the apology, were nothing short of speechless, while Myles, a blithe and ever-heedless human being, was quick to forgive the incident.

"No matter, Mrs. Academy. You and I are very much alike, you know!" he beamed.

"I'm grateful, Mr. Goodrich. If you'll now excuse me, honorable contributors, the Academy's team will be departing now." Without another word, the woman spun on her heel and departed. In mechanical swiftness, her associates opened their briefcases, stowed their equipment into perfectly sized compartments, and filed out of the office.

"I think we have some very worthy sleuthing companions," Myles announced.

Melissa and Calvin did not share the enthusiasm.

FIVE

"We shall not tolerate any more errors of the sort, Ms. McPherson."

"My team had no idea there would be any clues left to find."

"The entire purpose of your investigation was to assure that there would be no clues to find; that is the core definition of a detective's work! Had this slipped by us the murderer would be much harder to catch than he is now—but I think you comprehend the deeper issue."

"If you hadn't allowed Paragon—"

"I do hate to interrupt you, Ms. McPherson, but contrary to your estimation of my abilities, Kaufmann's acquisition of Paragon's services was entirely beyond my control. Indeed, they are a danger now, but until I am able to arrange for the termination of our partnership with them, you will learn to perform your duties in the presence of a superior detective!"

"You insult me, sir."

"A completely warranted insult, Ms. McPherson, considering today's events. In the meantime, we must do our best to utilize Paragon as an asset."

"Your point?"

"Ah, Demetria, as long as we get there first, it does not matter what Paragon says or does. It does not matter what they report to the miserable mayor of this miserable town."

"Sir, we have to solve the case. If you are suggesting that we let Paragon take credit for the work we accomplish—"

"But that's exactly what I am suggesting."

```
"We cannot do that, Mr. Powers. It's too
high of a risk."
"Not if your department steps up to the
plate and performs its job without
oversight."
"Goodnight, sir."
"Demetria!"
"What?"
"You must allow Paragon to believe they are
in control. Constrain their resources, make
the crime scene a controlled environment—a
playground! Control every variable, Ms.
McPherson. But never give them supremacy."
```

I.

MYLES GOODRICH SMILED, A BROAD GRIN ILLUMINATED BY THE GLOW of the streetlight. The snow had lightly resumed again, but this was a very important mission which would be hindered by no weather.

What neither Calvin nor Melissa could be trusted to do was assigned to Myles! While they labored away on the case, Myles the Magnificent Messenger would see to matters yet to be completed. He had been assigned the momentous task of delivering their discoveries to Kaufmann that evening. As he trudged along the slick pavement, a contented smile revealed a blithe unawareness of his coworkers' annoyed disposition towards him.

"It does seem rather inconsiderate of them to work on the case in my absence," Myles fantasied. "It is often me who has to point out the obvious details! They're always missing them."

Myles, of course, couldn't have understood Calvin and Melissa's ability to compute such details unspoken.

Presently, a distant roar thundered across the empty streets, a sound that one could almost always attribute to an Academy vehicle. The street in front of him began to light up as the headlights approached.

Myles expected the car to rip past him—to carefully veer into that large puddle on his left and send a wave of putrid ice-water rushing up to greet him. But the car did no such thing. It began to slow.

He cast a sideways glance at the massive, smoldering panther which rolled up to meet him. A surprising wave of heat struck his skin as the long, luxurious car came to a rumbling stop. The car was black, gilded in absolute darkness, crafted out of Night itself. His eyes rolled across the smooth, shadowy surface, beginning at the sharp, tapered rear and coming to rest at the silver insignia mounted proudly over the hood.

The grille glowed with a fiery hatred; a demon was contained within this metal cage. Nine shafts of metal, sharpened like double-edged swords, stood confidently inside this mouth of flame. If the other Academy vehicles were phantoms, surely this was Hades, the master of them all.

From the seat of the roofless carriage, a voice called: "Going my way?"

"Toward the Mayor's office, sir," Myles boasted, his exaggerated confidence sustaining his inflated self-importance.

There was a moment of silence. "Mighty fine vehicle you have," Myles added.

"She is a beauty, Master Goodrich. Step inside."

There was no handle on the seamless exterior, but Myles soon understood that it would not be necessary. Like liquid metal, a portion of the side melted and scurried away, retreating into the belly of the vehicle. Myles stepped inside slowly, and as he seated himself next to the driver, the outer shell reassembled itself.

As the car rumbled to life, as the fiery beast within began to vociferate its deep, infuriated roar, Myles cast another sidelong glance at the driver of the vehicle. He was an older gentleman in a sharp and angular black suit. Everything about the man proclaimed the utmost appearance of control, from the unique way he styled himself to the very facial expressions he bore. No surprise could ever disturb the command he held over his countenance—the man demonstrated an emotional concealment that rivaled Melissa herself.

"My name is Morgan Powers. You must be Melissa's assistant." His voice delivered an aura of subtle danger—here was a man not to be trifled with.

"I'm Myles Goodrich, sir! I'm a detective at Paragon PI."

Powers replied as one might to an over-enthusiastic child: "Yes, we know."

Smirking naïvely, Myles rested his naked hand over the edge of the roofless vehicle.

It was hot!

Myles swore as he jerked his arm away from the surface. Powers chuckled quietly. "I see you've become acquainted with the interesting nature of this vehicle, Master Goodrich."

Myles only groaned in response.

"We've made many discoveries at the Academy, Myles. Fantastic discoveries! All the energy within this car is powered by a perpetual motion machine, a furnace that runs off her own heat! The exterior of the car is consistently kept at a liquefying temperature, held together and manipulated through thousands of thimble-sized gravity generators!"

This was gibberish to Myles.

"It's interesting, the discoveries that are made in this dazzling world. The resources and the intelligence we've amassed is, of course, astounding, but science is unable to fit through the bottleneck of society. Can you imagine, Master Goodrich, if this vehicle was put onto the streets of a great city such as Anesthesia?"

"You'd be a lot richer," Myles muttered dryly.

"Matters would quickly get out of hand," Powers continued, undeterred. "Society is not capable of handling things it cannot understand. It must be spoon-fed before it can be given the crown roast. But today, to our horror, we realize we have spoon-fed our posterity *on crown roast*. We live in a greedy world with greedy people, Myles. And in the shortness of life, eternity is demanded."

The car, reaching its destination, performed a smooth U-turn so that City Hall stood behind them. Myles was wishing he had walked.

Powers sunk to an impassioned whisper. "There is an unspoken class system throughout the entire world, even in the nations that claim to be free. The classes are the Regulator, and the *Regulated*. You have a chance, Myles—a chance to take part in the future!"

The side of the car melted away. Myles clambered out.

"The world is changing, Master Goodrich. Are you ready?"

Myles turned to face his chauffeur. He turned to face this man who had challenged him like no man had ever challenged him before. He turned to face the ghostly, immaterial panther that had no real shape at all, only a fiery demon within.

And the smirking face of his driver disappeared in a blur of motion as the low, crouching vehicle sped deep into the night.

Six

"It's only a matter of time before another murder occurs and Paragon stumbles upon a new, critical discovery."

"Shall I never be pardoned for one negligible mistake?"

"Until Paragon is out of our midst, I cannot soften my judgement to consider that error negligible. As it so happens, it is one of the most troubling issues on my plate. Pruitt's entire department is searching for a way to handle this crisis in the courts."

"So I can't even be trusted to keep a pathetic three-person company in check?"

"We can no longer consider them as insignificant as you describe. I apologize for my harshness, Ms. McPherson, but we must transfer this matter into more capable hands for the time being. The longer they stay on the case, the more we will have to accelerate the Project."

"The Project is doomed, sir; we've already proven that it can't even work in a tiny community like Comatose."

"You aren't placing anything on the line. Surely you were aware of such risks?"

"This surpasses risk; this is suicide."

"Demetria, you have always had my trust and sincerity—it is why I have consulted you so frequently on these matters. Though circumstances have allowed your disillusionment to be understandable, I would ask that you now return the confidence I have invested in you. Have patience. Your second chance is not far off."

I.

TALL AND RESOLUTE, COMPROMISING IN NOT EVEN THE SLIGHTEST expression of his character, the invincible and statuesque Jarvis McCain sat enframed upon Melissa's desk. He existed there as a motivation, if not the very voice of discontent that inspired her to try harder.

In the eyes of her mind, though the actual Jarvis would do no such thing, she saw his inexpressive mouth twist into a condescending snarl, and with the ears of fantasy heard his voice echo over her work, "Surely you can do better!"

She shuddered, she blinked, and the vision was gone.

She did not know how to regard their relationship of late. Jarvis McCain had always been a momentous figure to her, but somehow, despite her direct familial ties—a distant one. He was a good man, incorruptible and virtuous. But in becoming so, he had lost the ability to be influenced by *anyone*. Not even a beloved daughter.

Their relationship now was strained—whether due to his overbearing assistance in her business or something deeper and intangible, Melissa could not say for certain. Jarvis's intentions were paternal—benign, even—but his aptitude for detective work blinded him to the harshness of his critiques. Melissa had not yet made her peace.

As she looked at that picture, she saw not a father, but a god. She saw what the common outsider might see in the picture: a courageous-looking man full of remorseless determination. Perhaps there was once a time when she knew her father, before her mother died. She respected him, and he her. But they respected each other! Like coworkers, like strangers!

Strangers?

"Murderer's been quiet, huh?"

She snapped out of her stupor and turned her head slowly toward the speaker. It was the kind of comment Myles would make, but the words came from Calvin, and the tone of his voice expressed an entirely different demeanor. He bore a look of profound understanding.

But he couldn't have known. Not about her father.

Melissa glanced at her watch before she responded. "It's about four o'clock."

"Some forty hours since Miss Brady was killed," Calvin answered quietly.

"I keep coming back to the murderer's confidence through it all. We're not dealing with a desperate man here, Calvin."

"Desperate for attention, perhaps!" Myles cried merrily from the other room.

Melissa and Calvin glanced at each other, frustrated.

"Listen, Melissa, I've been worrying about the motive. I'm not entirely sure one exists."

"There's always a motive, Calvin, unless you're suggesting our killer is some kind of automated slaughter machine."

"But everything seems to contradict itself!" Calvin cried. "Revenge? No, that doesn't work. I'd believe it without Brady's death, and I'd believe it without the tavern massacre. But together? No correlation!"

Melissa sighed. "There's no obvious correlation, that's for sure. But it doesn't mean there's no motive."

"I'd almost believe the man's entirely off his rocker, if you will—"

"He is insane. No one murders ten people and walks away with their mind intact."

Calvin coughed impatiently. "I meant insane in the more *animalistic* sense of the word, like how one might describe a directionless, sporadic madman. But we both agree that our killer most certainly has direction!"

"Because of the note."

"Exactly! Why would a directionless madman leave a message for Kaufmann?"

"But the people in the tavern? There was no message for them."

Calvin sat down in front of Melissa's desk, pondering. She watched his eyelids close; she watched his lips form the syllables of unintelligible words.

And with a sudden flurry of energy, Calvin's worried countenance changed. She watched his eyes suddenly open in bright realization. She watched his lips form an incredulous smile.

"Maybe," he whispered, "the people in the tavern *were* the message."

She knew her friend; she knew her coworker. She knew not to interrupt him now.

"That massacre in the tavern was an introduction. Their deaths taught us what to expect, a unique, unprecedented kind of death. At the time, of course, we reasoned that these 'murders' were only the result of some kind of accident or viral infection."

"But then Miss Brady died in the same way."

"But do you see the *contrast*? What happened to the regular drunkards now happens to the secretary of our Mayor! Whatever point our killer is trying to make, no one is exempt!"

Myles entered the room, holding the office's wireless telephone. "A call for you, Melissa."

Taking the device from his hand with an annoyed disposition, she stood up and spouted a hasty salutation:

"You've reached Paragon Private Investi—"

"Who's speaking?"

The voice, so wild and unlike any human sound Melissa had ever heard, sent her downward to her chair again. The caller could not have detected this reaction—but Calvin immediately suspected danger. What else could compromise Melissa's composure with such ease?

"You're—" her voice warbled; she stopped and tried again. "You're speaking with Melissa McCain, Senior Investigator at—"

"You have no idea what I've been through." The voice had reduced its savageness but still held an edge that Melissa took as evidence for the caller's statement.

"May I ask who is calling?"

"I need help, I need it bad."

Melissa frowned. She was a private investigator; this wasn't her job! "Sir, I'm not sure what I'll be able to do for you. Have you called the Police Dep—"

"No!" the voice rasped. Melissa pulled the phone away, and Calvin looked at her with newfound concern.

"Melissa, would you prefer me to...?"

"No, no, I can handle this." She placed the phone back to her ear, and prompted, "Sir, what can I do for you that the Police can't?"

There was a pause. "I need an intermediary."

Melissa paled. The inkling she had formulated of the caller's identity rose from the specters and became real, manifested in the very voice from the phone. The Murderer was here.

"Have you come to turn yourself in?" she asked, incredulity gaining her face.

Calvin stuttered and tried to jump in. "Melissa—"

She shushed him with a glance. The caller continued: "I can't live with this! They keep dying and it's my fault but it's only the voices telling me what to do, it's all deeper than anyone could ever know, I'm trapped, trapped, trapped! Help me! Please!"

"I will intercede between you and the Police. Where can I meet you?"

"Melissa!" Calvin exclaimed.

Not hearing this, the voice laid out the details. "There is a small park in the center of the traffic circle where Avenues Grande and Morpheus meet. Do you see it?"

Melissa nodded and whispered, "Yes."

"There is a bright red phone booth at the top of a hill in that park. Do you see it?"

She gave her quiet affirmation again.

"I am there."

The line died. But Melissa's enthusiasm had been reborn. Instantly, she was on her feet! Out the door Melissa ran, jacket left behind in her flurry.

"Melissa!" Calvin cried, racing after her. Myles was quick to follow.

There were a few cars on the street, but Melissa easily skirted around them. Already she could see the phone booth on the hill. Already she could see the waiting silhouette of her enemy.

"Melissa! Stop!"

If she stopped now, the killer would escape and all would be lost. And here was the hill; here was the phone booth!

She did not perceive the cries behind her. She did not hear Calvin cry out, warning her.

She only heard herself curse when she opened the phone booth, when a stranger's still-living corpse fell to the ground. The Murderer was not here.

"You fool, he never was," she whispered.

A noise came from the phone inside the booth. She grasped for it. It was the voice again, but this time—soft! beckoning!

"Goodbye, Melissa..."

She dropped the phone and began to run. But suddenly—a hissing noise—above her, below her, *inside* of her.

Walls of flame! All around her!

The world of silence erupted into unbearable volume—and just as suddenly, like a radio clicking off, no longer computed. All was quiet as a wave of heat closed in and lifted her into the sky, sending her higher and higher until it reached a terminal size, and then released her from its terrifying grip. She tumbled blindly down a hill of churning fire and smoke—every neuron in her body screamed meaningless reports of pain and damage, overwhelming her mind with sensory data.

And at last, unable to bear the heat any longer, Melissa succumbed to the sleep that desired her so deeply.

Falling, sinking, sleeping, comatose.

Seven

"Alive?"

"Barely, sir. She was able to move from the epicenter of the explosion, but she's still badly burned. We were unable to track down the perpetrator, but it's suspected the attack was commenced by some kind of propelled explosive."

"A rocket launcher?"

"Something of the type."

"Where is she now?"

"Intensive Care Unit, sir. They have her hooked up to life support. I tell you, she is *clinging* to life."

"We must be vigilant as we take care of her. If we allow the murderer to unplug her life support, she will most certainly die."

"We will send in an appropriate security presence, of course."

"Of course, Ms. McPherson. It's a shame though, that she now has to suffer."

"I would be rejoicing in her survival."

"I'm afraid, Ms. McPherson. The murderer has a tendency to remove whoever stands in his way. When this killer decides that one is worthy to die! Who will say otherwise?"

I.

"She will recover?" Calvin implored.

The doctor, an uninteresting character with a high forehead and bushy, concealing eyebrows, was not comfortable with such questions. He mulled over a number of responses to give to the young, dangerously curious man. Perhaps he might say, "Medicine is never an exact science; I do not know."

But that would place him in an unprofessional light. Perhaps he might say, "Haha, of course she will recover, go have a drink and come back tomorrow!"

But that would leave him liable for her complete recovery— an awkward situation the doctoral community of Comatose consciously avoided. *It would be unspeakable to be held responsible for the things that came out of my mouth!* he thought. *Better to not speak at all.*

The doctor voiced none of those things. "Burns take time to heal, young man. But she is a spirited young gal. But you must be patient, she will be unconscious for an indefinite amount of time."

The doctor did not like to speak. He did not like to raise hope or lower it. Such expressions of encouragement were too liable.

And Calvin? Here lay his friend of old, the coworker who had shaped him into the investigator he was today. Here she lay on a white bed, wrapped in gauze. Everything human about her wandered between ventilator machines and cardiac monitors.

He recalled the happiest moment he had shared with her— captured in a small picture frame that hung above the entrance to Paragon's offices. Within the frame sat a photo of the three investigators, taken just a year prior at a small company picnic in the peaceful forests above the town. Calvin, Melissa, and Myles, all laughing at some long forgotten jest in a bygone time of happiness.

He recalled the explosion. In the blink of an eye, everything he had appreciated about his dear friend was thrown into the air with her. He could not close his eyes—not without seeing that bright fireball that surrounded his friend.

But now, something else surrounded Melissa, a black, nebulous cloud of death and mystery. And here she lay on a white bed, the key to their enigma locked within her mind. The cloud, desperate to snuff out her candle—and with it, extinguish the truth.

Presently, the doctor was asking Calvin to leave, to let her be alone, to rest.

He was asking him to say goodbye, to abandon her, to damn her to cope with the cloud of death...

II.

It was dark in the hospital when she awoke.

Not a muscle in her body could be convinced to move; the agony was far too great. But her brain needed no encouragement. The silence was severe and the questions many.

"Where am I?" she wondered. "Who put me here?"

And after those initial inquiries regarding her location went unanswered, she tried turning her attention to her surroundings. But everything was confusing, all of these shapes were wrong, all of these shadows were unearthly and strange.

Including that one.

And it dawned on her: *that* shadow was perhaps the one material thing in her room. It moved like a human and maintained its form. Her eyes followed this dark mass as it approached her.

A hand appeared, thrust from the shadows. It was gloved in white velvet, like a doctor, perhaps. But this was wrong, this was no doctor. Here was the soft, beckoning voice. This was wrong, this was no doctor!

"It is the violent hand that deals death, Melissa. But sleep? Sleep comes from a soft touch."

The hand hovered on the illuminated display of the ventilator.

And then there were no more lights. The glove retreated into darkness.

And the darkness advanced on her.

EIGHT

"I've received word from the hospital, sir."
"Yes?"
"Melissa McCain, sir. She was found dead this morning."
"The cause?"
"It seems her ventilator had been shut off."
"Shut off? In what manner? Did it malfunction?"
"No, sir. The doctors reactivated the machine and found it perfectly functional. It's suspected that the machine's deactivation was deliberate."
"This is unfortunate. I considered her to be one of Paragon's finest investigators. There is, you say, no chance that she turned it off herself? Could it have been bumped earlier in the day?"
"She was hardly in condition to reach across the bed. As to your second question, do you really believe that a machine as important as a ventilator could be so easily disabled?"
"I suppose not. Has Paragon responded to the death?"
"That is the other news I need to share with you, sir. Paragon and Kaufmann have agreed that immediate measures must be taken. Kaufmann has called for an emergency hearing of the City Council this morning."
"What!"
"They want to propose a state of emergency. They want to engage investigators from the Initiative in Anesthesia."
"Who will be representing Paragon before the City Council?"

"Myles Goodrich, sir."
"Ah. Not Mr. Calvin Barker?"
"He's out of town, sir. He felt obligated
to inform Jarvis McCain about his
daughter's decease."
"This may work in our favor. But what of
our allies in the council?"
"Allies, sir?"
"Honestly, Demetria! You have your liberals
and your conservatives—how many members are
in the *Academy Party*?"
"We only have a minority in the council as
of last election."
"The rest can be...persuaded. This action
must not move forward. I shall attend this
meeting myself. There is no margin for
error here."

I.

Now the Comatose assembly chamber was one of the finest offices of the city hall. Housed in a smaller building adjacent to the warehouse, the headquarters of the City Council seemed only to exist as a boastful thorn in Kaufmann's side. The chamber, which also functioned as a courtroom, was paneled with dark wood and carried a clean, imperial look.

The city council, of course, afforded these luxuries. These men and women had a rather different view on their position in government. Unlike Kaufmann, who begrudgingly accepted his job out of obligation, these councilors enjoyed their job.

They enjoyed knowing that all of their oversights could be blamed on the mayor.

Kaufmann, who was already seated behind the bench, carefully watched their procession into the room. There was not a single man or woman in the council whom he trusted. Thirteen of them, all callous and corrupt.

The councilors sat at a semi-circular desk facing him. Five of the councilors, Kaufmann noted quickly, wore white suits. Fastened to their lapels was a silver pin bearing a capital "*A*." And if this wasn't subtle enough, they all sat together at one end of the desk, wearing their typical knowing smiles.

Behind the councilors were more desks, which were sparsely filled with administrative assistants and other required members of the meeting. Empty desks boasted delusions of grandeur—wrought and woven with ambition, yet vacant.

As the doors to the room began to close, Mr. Morgan Powers of the Academy entered. He was dressed in a caped overcoat and walked with calm, measured steps. Kaufmann unconsciously drew his suit jacket tighter. By Powers's mere presence, all things bright and warm seemed to cringe and cower before his authority.

As Powers sat down at a desk behind the five white-suited councilors, Kaufmann suddenly felt very opposed. The Academy did not want this measure to move forward.

And the Academy usually got their way.

To Kaufmann's right was Myles Goodrich, representing Paragon PI. To Kaufmann's left was Theophilus Patel, Speaker of the Council. He was a short man in a crisp, well-fitting suit, and when one noted his prim, nervous conduct and his long, beak-like nose, he bore a striking resemblance to a penguin. When silence fell around the room, Patel rose and addressed the crowd.

"Mayor Kaufmann, Councilors of the City of Comatose, ladies, gentlemen." The voice, contrary to the owner's appearance, was broad and soothing, accustomed to the confines of echoey halls and assembly rooms. "We are gathered today to discuss the necessity of peacekeeping and investigative assistance from the Global Cooperation Initiative in the suspected serial homicides that have taken place within our city limits."

Patel paused. Some quiet murmurings among the councilors became audible, but these were silenced as the Speaker continued.

"This emergency hearing, as requested by Mayor Kaufmann, must reach a verdict by the end of the day. To expedite this, we will do away with some of the usual decorum and proceed immediately. I now would like to welcome up Mr. Myles Goodrich of Paragon Private Investigations."

Patel moved to the side and primly folded his hands behind him. Myles, fearlessly, rose and took the floor.

"Good morning," he began with a smile.

There was a prolonged silence in the room. Someone coughed.

Myles laughed nervously before continuing. "My name is Myles Goodrich. I'm the senior investigator at Paragon PI." This, of course, was false. "Many of you may be wondering, well, 'What the hell is Paragon?'"

Myles chuckled, but no one laughed with him. He resumed, with a little less confidence:

"Ah...well. We are a private investigative firm working on the solving of this—" (here he carefully read from his notes) "*serial homicide*. Quite a mouthful, eh?"

Silence again. One of the white-suited councilors rose in his seat. There was a sudden movement from Patel, who addressed the disruption. "Councilor Hewitt, a question?"

"Yes, for Mr. Goodrich, please."

"I'm listening!" Myles cried.

"Er, yes, thank you," Councilor Hewitt began. "The investigation of serial homicide is not a task commonly undertaken by small, private firms such as yourselves. Might I inquire as to who engaged your services?"

Myles's earnestness to be of use overpowered his sense of caution. "We were hired by Mr. Samuel Kaufmann, seated behind me. He was unhappy with the way the Acad—"

Myles stopped, his gaffe realized too late. Kaufmann concealed his face in his palms—Mr. Goodrich was spoiling their chances.

Councilor Hewitt smiled thinly and seated himself. Myles, momentarily embarrassed, resumed with his previous demeanor. "Many of you may be aware of the murders at *The Charming Highwayman* a few days ago. Nine persons were killed—"

"Yes, Councilor Stafford?" Patel announced.

A white-suited woman stood. "Are there any other firms actively collaborating with Paragon on this investigation? And if so, shouldn't they be represented here as well?"

Kaufmann, before Myles could answer, remarked hurriedly, "That question is irrelevant to the subject matter at this time, Councilor Stafford."

Patel raised his eyebrows with something akin to alarm. "Is this question of interest to the council as a whole?"

The five white-suited councilors stood in unison. And, following some furtive glances, the rest of the council also rose.

"If you please, Mr. Goodrich," Patel murmured.

Too late, Myles realized the snare he had stumbled into.

"Uh...well, I am bound to discretion, Mr. Speaker—"

"So why did you answer the question regarding your employer?" Councilor Stafford demanded.

"Speaking out of turn, Councilor Stafford," Patel said, out of habit. In actuality, he concurred with the logic behind the outcry.

"Mr. Goodrich," Patel prompted, "the original question raised by Councilor Stafford is crucial to determining the council's course of action."

"The other investigative firm is the Academy," Myles muttered.

With a triumphant swell of her voice, Councilor Stafford cried, "Mr. Patel, I demand that this other firm be represented behind the bench."

Patel then announced, "Are there any in this assembly who can represent the Academy?"

Kaufmann watched, with mounting terror, as a regal figure near the back of the room rose from his chair and addressed the panel.

"I am Morgan Powers, Executive Chairman of the Academy."

"Mr. Powers, will you come to the floor?" Patel asked. Powers made his way to the bench, where he sat next to Myles' chair.

"I will now have Mr. Goodrich continue his narration, and will ask of the audience that no more interruptions occur until after he has finished," Patel announced.

Myles's humor had been effectively squashed by the most recent turn of events. With a defeated mumble, he finished it out:

"After the deaths at the tavern, an assistant to Mr. Kaufmann was killed in the same way. And yesterday," Myles said, his voice rising, "my assistant, Melissa McCain, was wounded in a deliberate explosion and subsequently killed in her sleep at the hospital!"

There were some loud murmurs in the crowd.

"We at Paragon believe that these deaths are intentional and related. Therefore, as the killer has crippled our department, we are convinced that neither Paragon nor the Academy is capable of continuing the investigation."

Myles held his notes up to his eyes as he slowly read off the final paragraph:

"We at Paragon PI believe that a state of emergency must be declared for the City of Comatose. Action must be taken to stop this terrorism at all costs. We also believe that the safest, most impartial course of action at this time would be to engage an outside investigator from the Global Cooperation Initiative to conduct the concluding examinations. Thank you."

Myles seated himself as the room echoed with loud objections.

"The Academy is the most respectable establishment in the city!"

"A GCI investigator! The expenditure would be extraordinary!"

"This is outrageous! The facts are misconstrued!"

For a good span of time, Patel stood like a child before a tumultuous ocean, using his perceived magic skills to subdue the wave, to silence the crowd. No loudness of voice nor gesture of hand would quiet these councilors!

When the impassioned arguments had simmered slightly, he raised his voice one last time so as to continue the hearing. "The proposed action would be to declare a state of emergency and to engage a professional investigator from the Global—"

Councilor Stafford, still standing, opposed him with a haughty retort. "Another account must be given! Mr. Goodrich has not convincingly detailed the 'inadequacies' of the Academy's distinguished forensics team."

"Is it in the interest of the council as a whole to hear from Mr. Powers?" Patel asked.

This time, all thirteen members stood in one accord.

"I now introduce Mr. Powers to the floor," Patel said.

Powers rose with the leisure and certainty of an ascending skyscraper. "The cause for alarm," he began with a soft, confident voice, "is perfectly understandable. After all, these incidents have indeed been alarming and worrisome. However, this commotion is unwarranted: The danger itself is misunderstood. Allow me a minute to detail the facts that our investigators have independently gathered."

The crowd clung to Powers' words like a child to the cliffhanger of a fireside story.

"The nine 'deaths' in the tavern, of course, were not really murders at all. In fact, these nine are not, clinically speaking, *even dead*. The same is true with Miss Brady, the Mayor's assistant. The ten, who Paragon maintains were 'killed,' are currently in the hospital, alive and well, preserved in what doctors would call a *persistent vegetative state*."

"But there was a murderer!" Kaufmann cried. "He left a note on my desk after Miss Brady died!"

Powers looked at him with a deep, unreadable expression. "It seems, Mr. Kaufmann, that you are misinformed. Our Forensics Department has discerned no correlation between the note and a potential suspect."

"Please, be seated, Mr. Kaufmann," Patel said.

"The decease of Melissa McCain is a more recent and unrelated case of most definite homicide. And since this death has absolutely no connection to the previous phenomena, I would advise the council to vote against this senseless 'necessity' for outside assistance."

He eyed the members of the bench, specifically Myles, with an air of compassion. "Though Paragon has taken a ghastly hit, and we mourn their loss grievously, it in no way undermines the competency of *our* Forensics team, which will deal with these matters in the swiftest fashion fate will allow."

MATTHEW ROBERTS | 47

There was silence—not the kind the follows an awkward remark—the kind that follows stunning, indisputable truth.

"The council must now decide," Patel announced. "Those in favor of the course of action proposed by Mr. Goodrich, please rise."

And there were thirteen occupied chairs in the assembly room.

NINE

"It was fortunate, I think, that it was not Calvin Barker who represented Paragon this morning."

"Your arguments were superb, sir. Even Mr. Pruitt congratulated your caution."

"A man after my own heart, Harrison Pruitt. But I owe some of the success to Ms. Stafford and Mr. Hewitt. I probably wouldn't have been able to speak if not for their actions."

"What is our next step, sir?"

"This, you must understand, is a battle on many fronts. Our first problem is this: Paragon is still championed by Kaufmann. In court we have maintained that these incidents were not murders. But if another attack should happen, Paragon will regain their traction, and we, the Academy, will be at a loss."

"Is that...avoidable, sir?"

"Strictly speaking, it is not. It's obvious to Kaufmann and the others that we are using these incidents to gain political leverage. But, strictly speaking again, we are merely taking advantage of an favorable situation. The perpetrator is quite likely to strike us, next."

"Forgive me for my insensitivity, sir, but if the perpetrator attacked us, would that also lower suspicion on us?"

"Yes, Ms. McPherson. Yes, it would."

I.

NOW THERE WAS A QUIET GRAVEL ROAD WHICH AMBLED THROUGH THE forested hills above Comatose. The road was not easy to find, but once discovered, the path took its passenger to high places from which could be seen the entirety of Dormido Valley. Situated in this valley, now looking smaller than ever before, was the town of Comatose.

The valley was tight, sharp, and small, and the hills that surrounded it were mostly untouched. There were no openings within the towering walls—Comatose lay completely circumscribed between the mountains of a city-wide hermitage.

This quiet, gravel road, a road which carried a man into the hills and out of the sleeping city, was one of the few routes of escape. Here in the hills, one could be alone with his thoughts, stimulated by the refreshing, arousing atmosphere, freed from the constricted self-interests of an indifferent city.

Calvin Barker glanced down at the city of ants below. In the incessant search for the elusive murderer, his quest had led him here, to this very view. Behold the city before him! Within he might find one ant who was not an ant at all; he would find a wasp hiding there.

Amidst the thick undergrowth of the hills, his eye caught the faintest glimpse of a red brick pillar obscured within the leaves. Calvin pulled off the path and glanced with interest at this small portal of civilization. He crossed the empty road. Between two ivy-covered pillars stood a green, wrought iron gate, and atop each pillar sat brass lions with one paw raised in a cautious fashion. Calvin strode to one of the pillars and brushed some of its leaves aside. Here he found another brass embellishment, a plaque which told him the number of the house.

451 Quiet Gravel Road. He was at the right address.

The gate was unlocked. Calvin admitted himself quietly. Before him, a tranquil creek ran across his path, but a humble, befitting bridge made the crossing quite simple. Around the corner Calvin came, finding himself before the McCain Estate. A long, simple lawn stretched on either side of the stone pathway, manicured effortlessly by gardening machines.

The manor, shrouded behind a thick wall of rosebushes and backdropped by the woods beyond the property, boasted of a grandeur that could not be predicted from the humble gate he had entered. Tucked away in the trees sat a large country house, three stories tall. The building, contrary to the modern structures of the cities, was built many years prior with red bricks and pronounced bay windows.

Calvin crept toward the door. His host was certainly cordial, but the approachability ended there. Companionship could never exist between a normal man and Jarvis—jokes and jests, smiles and friendship—they simply fell on deaf ears. A solemn life was that of Jarvis McCain, and few could live it so flawlessly.

Calvin raised the brass knocker three times. At first, there was silence. But then, footsteps could be heard inside and after a moment's hesitation, the man within opened the door.

Jarvis was tall—not abnormally so—but neither was he at eye-level. He had neat grey hair, parted to the right with cognizant precision. His mustache was trimmed in a similar fashion, not a whisker out of line. He wore a crisp pair of rimless reading glasses, modern and rectangular.

Though robed in a thick dressing gown, Calvin detected underneath a button-down shirt and dark pants—a sign of vigilance, perhaps. Here was a man who would never be seen in his pajamas.

There was a thin smile of recognition.

"Mr. Barker. It's been quite some time since I've seen you." The voice was clear and authoritative.

"Please, come in," Jarvis continued.

"Thank you, Mr. McCain," Calvin replied, noting already the respect his mind had unconsciously supplemented.

The room was furnished in the modern-antique fusion that Calvin was beginning to associate with Jarvis, despite misleading outward appearances. The furniture had an aluminum theme, which brightened the room sharply. On the wall was a large television screen, tuned to the news station from Anesthesia.

Comatose did not have a news station.

Jarvis was well acquainted with the way his guest glanced at the room. Calvin's eyes rolled over every minute detail of the house, gathering information, collecting what he could about his host.

"Living out here, one might wonder how I get any news at all," Jarvis smiled. "But as it turns out, I am better informed than the entire town of Comatose."

Calvin was not one for smalltalk, and he knew that Jarvis would run out of words even faster.

"You may be wondering why I am here, sir," Calvin murmured. "I have some troubling news for you."

"Let's hear it then," Jarvis growled. He walked over to what appeared to be a plain, aluminum box in the center of the room. On top of this box were a set of handles, and upon pulling these apart, a tray of refrigerated drinks rose from within.

"I have some troubling news," Calvin repeated. "You may want to sit down, sir."

Jarvis looked almost startled, but he maintained his composure.

"Melissa?" his voice rasped.

"She's dead, sir."

For some time, Jarvis stood there, a statue. Calvin watched his face. Something had shifted, and Calvin could see it. The incorruptible Jarvis had a crack in his armor, and inside the unchanging shell a human would be found, terrified and regretful.

Jarvis made a move for the tray of refreshments. His previous intention was to pour a glass of water, for he rarely partook in alcohol. But now his hand grasped a small pitcher of Cognac.

When he finally spoke, he could not bring himself to directly address Melissa's death.

"I am troubled, Mr. Barker, that *you* had to bring this information to me. Where are your policemen?"

"We have five officers, half of what our town needs. And of these five, three are off at a time."

Jarvis nodded, neither incredulous nor intrigued. He tried to pour the brandy, but his hands were trembling and he spilled over the tray. Calvin stepped forward and filled a glass for the man.

Jarvis sat down. He smiled—an angry smile, by which his iron brows caved inward with calculated angles of rage, illuminating a fierce gleam in those sad yet vigilant eyes. "And to think, that if you had not been able to bring me this news, why!" A tremor of rage gripped his hand, and the liquor rolled upward from the glass and splashed forth again. "Months might've passed before I..."

"We believe she was killed, sir."

Jarvis scowled. He carefully took a drink. "By whom?"

"We think it was the murderer that Kaufmann hired us to find," Calvin answered.

Jarvis glanced out the window, restless, and then rose from his seat to continue his contemplation. Calvin watched the older man but made no further comments.

His gaze still directed toward some point on the horizon, Jarvis raised a new question. "How did she die?"

The bright, loathsome fireball, hurling Melissa's fragile body straight off the earth and into oblivion, flashed through Calvin's mind and barred him from response. But when Jarvis met his gaze with those perceptive, unreadable eyes, the reluctance withered away.

Calvin sighed in dismal devastation. "After receiving a call from our killer that supposedly divulged his location, Melissa ran, without our consent, to meet and apprehend the man. She was gravely wounded by an explosion when she arrived. But it... well it seemed like she might recover. But..." Calvin trailed off, his lip erupting into uncontrollable tremors.

Jarvis passed the Cognac.

"...She, uh—they found her dead at the hospital the next morning," Calvin whispered. "Her ventilator had been externally shut off."

Jarvis simply nodded. There were no words to be said. For some time the men sat in silence and pondered the ill fate of a friend, a daughter, a good human being. Melissa, in that very moment, came back to life in the passionate maelstrom of happy memories in which she yet dwelt. Jarvis thought of the swingset, wherein the child sat giggling as he pushed her peacefully back and forth, back and forth. Calvin thought of the picnic, where he had sat amongst companions in these very hills and never dreamt that such a horrid fate would befall his friend.

Must this evil world perpetually demand its best?

"The last time I saw Melissa," Jarvis murmured, "was not a happy time for either of us. She had told me of Paragon's recent financial troubles, and I offered her some advice—but I was too critical! I wish she had allowed me to clarify my opinion...I meant no insult to her way of business. But she left in an angry flurry, and I never worked up the courage to ask her pardon. Now I shall never get that chance."

Calvin had never seen the man so distraught. Another long silence transpired, and as he watched Jarvis, it became clear that a new topic of discussion must be opened—or the quietude would exist indefinitely.

A murmur trickled from the old man's throat. "Tell me about your murderer."

Calvin tossed a startled glance at the elder, but obliged. "Melissa's death was an anomaly. The last ten victims were inexplicably placed into irreversible comas. Outside of that, we have no clue."

"Fascinating," Jarvis breathed. "I've never heard of such a thing."

"I find it abhorrent," Calvin retorted. "Condemning someone to a fate like that...enduring existence without end, eternal confinement to that wasteland between sleep and wakefulness...I could never force someone to that fate. For Melissa's sake, I need to find—"

Jarvis's head snapped forward. "Listen!" he cried, his attention directed away from Calvin's commentary. He flicked his wrist in an upward flourish and his television, like an orchestra responding to its conductor, surged in volume.

"...a massive new university. The Global Cooperation Initiative today authorized the construction near the center of

Anesthesia. This university is actually a satellite campus of the Academy, an internationally acclaimed private institution based in the Dormido Valley area. The establishment is expected to see completion in a few years from now..."

"What does your Academy want in Anesthesia?" Jarvis mused.

To Calvin there seemed to be a striking irrelevance in the question. Did the old man even care that the murderer was still loose in Comatose—or that the selfsame villain had brought about his daughter's death? "Mr. McCain, I'm obligated to solve this mystery once and for all! I can't concern myself with the Academy's antics elsewhere when I'm facing a terrorist situation *right here.*" Calvin cried.

Jarvis's eyebrows rose conspicuously. "It is that kind of ignorance, Mr. Barker, that will bring ruin to Comatose."

Calvin's initial, autonomous respect to the elder felt cheapened by the criticism. "What makes you think so?"

"You must be wary, my friend, of the assumptions you make. The first: You have created the notion that the citizens of Comatose are *aware* of their plight, and are *concerned* about it."

"How could they—"

"After years, Mr. Barker, *years* of facing the expansion of tolerance and liberalism, do you believe people truly care anymore? Initially they showed bigotry and hatred, but society kept shoving more and more things for them to accept! The people withdrew, concerned themselves with only their own affairs, and became silent inhabitants of the world that turned a deaf ear to reason. You cannot force them to care about your problem—not even when it may endanger them."

"I respect that you've garnered a broad knowledge of politics, sir," Calvin muttered, "but *my* problem has nothing to do with that—I need to find this killer." Calvin stood to leave.

Jarvis performed a careful examination of the young man. "Be wary, Mr. Barker," he repeated. "Do not assume you can so easily isolate your murders from the bigger picture."

From Calvin he received a brief nod, a handshake, and a word of gratitude. The younger man fastened his coat and opened the door back into the world. Jarvis did not rise from his chair to bid him farewell.

"Will you be alright, sir?" he asked.

"Let's hope so."

"What about the murderer, sir?" Calvin asked. "I have no indication of where he'll strike next."

Jarvis eyed him with a peculiar gleam. "I speak out of prudence, not arrogance, when I say this: I will not be affected. Your killer is one who preys on the unprepared. And believe me, Mr. Barker—there are very few in Comatose who are ready for what will come of this."

TEN

"The murderer has spared us another day."

"You sound disappointed, sir."

"Do I? In context of the city's suspicion, I am disappointed. The murderer is obviously trying to draw attention to our lack of victims. He may indeed be framing us for his deeds."

"That does put us in a rather disagreeable position."

"Well, well. We must solve this ourselves."

"Sir? Are you suggesting we murder our own?"

"No! We have too many resources to resort to something so primitive."

"What are you suggesting, then?"

"Have Doctor Vescovi and his coworkers moved to Deep Storage until further notice. You'll be filing a conclusive Forensics Report on their 'death.'"

"But they will live, sir?"

"There are approximately seventy employees whose criminal charges took them to Deep Storage. Embezzlement of government funds, corporate espionage, all of our mistakes. They're happily continuing their employment downstairs."

"Isn't that...illegal, sir?"

"I suppose it is. Why do you ask?"

I.

CALVIN.

Had not seen Myles in three days.

Though he had sent several calls, all he received back were vague excuses to terminate the conversation as quickly as possible.

The elusive nature of his coworker was not entirely surprising, but he knew that something must soon change: Paragon could not continue functioning like a one-man show.

Entering the office after yet another fruitless search of the city archives, Calvin cast a wary glance toward Melissa's desk. Not one paperweight had moved since her death, of course. To disrupt such a sacred place would be blasphemy—an unspeakable sin! But her desk was a shrine of inspiration now. There Calvin could sit, and perhaps hear the faint echoes of his friend's brilliance...

He cast a thorough gaze over the superficial layer of papers on the desk. There were some forensic reports from the Academy, quite a few contrasting reports that Melissa had composed herself, and a great deal of notes and sketches.

"For the sake of the case," Calvin murmured. "I must."

These files were vital; the sacred shrine would have to be disrupted. Respectfully, he began to leaf through the papers. From beneath a hefty chemical analysis report, a dog-eared page caught his eye.

He lifted it up to the window's light. On the paper was written PERSONS OF INTEREST, and underneath were several names. She had crossed out names such as Kaufmann, but the list contained several city councilors and...

"Morgan Powers?" Calvin voiced aloud.

Myles, the prodigal son, suddenly entered the main room from the inner office. He had a nervous look about him—could there be a reason he had begun avoiding Calvin so desperately?

"Oh! Calvin! I didn't hear you come in."

Calvin glanced up at his coworker. The man looked tired and defeated—an appearance Calvin had never expected to see on Myles Goodrich.

"What happened to you?" Calvin asked.

"Oh, it was awful, Calvin! The proposal the other day couldn't have gone worse!"

The proposal. Calvin had quite forgotten that it had been Myles' job to represent Paragon in the emergency hearing of the City Council. His surprise at seeing Myles turned into fear—fear that this unaddressed mishap would cost them dearly.

"What happened, Myles? I could have sworn the Council was scared to death on the matter."

"Everything was going fine, until one councilor stood up and demanded that the Academy be represented in the hearing."

"And?"

"Well, lo and behold! Isn't it convenient that Mr. Morgan Powers happens to be sitting in? He comes up to the stage and starts talking smooth! Curse it all, Calvin! Morgan Powers, chief of the Academy, goes up there and claims that the victims were not murdered at all!"

Calvin had never seen Myles this upset. And the man had every right to be. This was not supposed to happen! Calvin specifically put Myles on the assembly because the ruling was a no-brainer!

But suddenly, out of nowhere, the Academy arrives with unprecedented influence and sways the Council in the complete opposite direction. Why?

"So we're on our own," Calvin voiced aloud.

"There was something off, Calvin. The whole thing seemed planned."

The phone suddenly rang. Myles ran off to fetch it, but the sound was not coming from the inner office. Calvin glanced down at Melissa's desk, where the wireless receiver lay, ringing.

Untouched since delivering the call that ended Melissa's life...

Calvin, with a deep inhalation to hush a burst of grief in his chest, picked up the phone. Myles, elucidated to the phone's whereabouts, returned to watch.

"Mr. Barker, perhaps?" an tranquil, authoritative voice inquired.

"Yes, you've reached Paragon Private Investigations. Can I help you?"

"This is Morgan Powers, Executive—"

"Alright. Do you have information for us?" Calvin was fed up will all the decorum and suffixes—he wanted answers.

Myles furrowed his brow and tilted his head at a slight angle, as if to pose a question. Calvin mouthed the name of the caller and returned to the conversation.

"As a matter of fact," Mr. Powers replied, "I have some alarming developments from our Chemistry Department. It's rather urgent, I'm afraid."

"Let's hear it, then."

"I needn't go into the logistics of our privacy policies, Mr. Barker, but as a Class I incident—"

"You're not obliged to speak of it over the phone," Calvin finished.

"Precisely, sir," Powers returned, his cordial tone betraying no frustration. "I've arranged an opening to meet with you in half an hour at my office."

"I'll be there. What floor?"

"There will be a secretary to show you in. Good day, Mr. Barker."

Calvin set the phone down and glanced at Myles. "I apparently have an appointment with Mr. Powers."

II

THE ELEVATOR WHICH RAN UP THE SIDE OF THE ACADEMY'S MAIN building was glass in construction. Within, as it climbed higher into the sky, Calvin could see all of Comatose once more. But something was different this time. From his visit in the mountains with Jarvis he saw a calm, peaceful town—a refreshing view, a relaxing view.

From the glass elevator he saw quite a different city. Now he felt like the general of some power-hungry army, looking upon his battlefield. He was no longer far enough away from the town to see its beauty. From the glass elevator he was close enough to see everything as it was: deplorably hopeless.

The glass elevator stopped. Calvin entered a broad antechamber paneled with dark mahogany. The interiors were furnished in the most imperial yet contemporary fashion possible, calling to mind the regal essence of Morgan Powers, a man who deserved the fear and reverence of all who encountered him.

Calvin, whether in blithe pride or simple imprudence, had no concept of it.

The secretary who had admitted him silently gestured to the end of the room. She had no intention of following him there. Between two pillars of black marble bespeckled with pebbles of pearl stood a vast set of gilded mahogany doors, one of which was ajar. Calvin would not allow this sumptuous display of power to unnerve him. He moved onward with resolute confidence, barely hearing the whisper of the elevator as it returned to the lobby.

Inside, Calvin expected to see the man busily working. Instead he found Powers amusing himself with a Newton's cradle.

"Mr. Barker. Have a seat, if you will," Powers beckoned.

Calvin glanced about the expansive room. The ceiling rose nearly three stories high, where it suddenly curved up into a towering glass spire. Calvin hadn't realized that they were, indeed, at the very pinnacle of the building. There were no floors above Powers' office.

The room was surprisingly bright; Calvin had not expected a man like Powers to keep his office—if one could call it that—in such an atmosphere. The room's immensity and lack of unnecessary furniture defined it differently in Calvin's mind. A studio, perhaps?

A throne room?

In silent reverence at the grandeur before him, Calvin slid a chair across a floor of seamless black marble until he was closer to Powers' desk.

"Finance and Internal Affairs," Mr. Powers declared. Calvin raised an eyebrow at this odd conversation starter, but terminated the body language upon understanding that the comment had been directed to a voice-activated intercom.

"Mr. Pruitt's office, Priority One," Powers continued. A voice met him immediately:

"At your service, Mr. Powers."

"Ah, Harrison. You'll excuse me for troubling you," Powers asked.

"I have a moment to spare. What do you need?"

"Standby to declassify yesterday's Forensics report."

"Yes, sir."

Calvin glanced at Powers with confusion, but quite quickly he understood what Powers was doing—moments before the man decided to explain it to him.

"This murderer has proven to be most prevailing. We've had to protect our most important developments with dual-security measures."

Calvin watched Powers enter his credentials into the system and subsequently dismiss his associate.

"Secure the room," Powers spoke aloud.

In accordance with his wish, massive, semi-translucent curtains—like frosted glass—unfurled over the towering windows. The room significantly darkened. A three-dimensional figure appeared in the middle of the office, the image of an unfamiliar man.

"Is this...the murderer?" Calvin inquired, incredulous.

"Ha! If only. No, Mr. Barker, this man is an employee at our Chemistry Department. This is Dr. Octavio Vescovi, our lead chemist on the case."

"Why are you showing me his picture instead of his work?" Calvin asked.

"Because," Powers sighed, "He's dead. Along with two of his most prominent coworkers."

Calvin was stunned. This was the first he had heard of these deaths.

"Were they...killed? Like the others?"

"Yes. We've been anticipating the murderer's arrival for some time now. After all, what can one do?" Powers sighed.

"What were they working on?"

The man seemed more distressed than Calvin had ever seen him. Powers spoke as though he was alone in the room and Calvin had never asked any questions. "Dr. Vescovi and his associates were the only chemists working on the case...that is why they were killed. The murderer could not allow them to reveal their finished work to the world..."

"What was their work?" Calvin repeated.

Powers' eyes snapped to meet Calvin's. "A poison, Mr. Barker. A poison that would perfectly recreate the effects of the murderer's secret weapon."

From a vault within his desk, Powers withdrew a box of smooth, dark metal. And delicately, as if the world was contained inside, he lifted a brilliant glass globe to meet Calvin's eyes.

The globe shone with an eerie luster. Shafts of its own light burst forth in terrible beauty, casting the dark room in a sinister, deep red atmosphere. Incredulity filled Calvin's mind—here lay an artifact more precious than rubies, for its wealth was not merely in the eye of the beholder, but in its deadly power.

"The concoction within this globe reproduces the effects of the murderer's weapon—exactly," Powers whispered proudly.

His mind beheld the contrivance with reverent wonder.

Isn't it beautiful, Calvin?

Shaking his head violently, he posed a predictable question upon his host: "Why does it glow like that?"

Powers sighed. "I do not know, nor do any of our chemists. It will take them weeks to catch up to the work Dr. Vescovi left behind. There was but one thing Vescovi had not discovered in this poison."

"Which was?"

"How the murderer covered his tracks. In all the test animals, the chemists easily tracked down the traces of the poison we fed them. But in the real victims, we found nothing," Powers said, regret lacing his voice.

"Perhaps I could find something." Calvin blinked, then reaffirmed his desire with a brisk nod. "I could help."

A shade of doubt crossed the other's face. He drew the radiant globe closer.

It is beautiful, Calvin!

"I need it, sir. If ever you wanted to end these murders, give it to me. Please."

Calvin almost believed the words he was speaking.

Powers cast a shrewd glance of intrigue at Calvin, and then conceded. He placed the brilliant globe in its box. "So be it. As your coworker, I am obliged to share with you everything we discover.

Perhaps, Mr. Barker, you will be able to see something that we missed."

The box closed. The erratic passion driving Calvin onward dissolved into a blur of confusion. The beauty of the orb, now confined to his memory alone, seemed diminished and feeble—had it truly been as magnificent as he just so recently believed?

Calvin, with bewildered resolution, accepted the dark, metallic box from the other man's hand and wondered how useful the treasure within would actually be to him. But to betray this sudden hesitation would be an unbearable cowardice! His cheeks inflated in a reassuring smile.

"Thank you for your time, Mr. Barker," Powers concluded, turning his attention toward the security curtains, which began to ascend at the snap of his fingers. Calvin took this as a cue to leave—he needed time to contemplate the object that had so carelessly fallen into his hands.

The marbled antechamber, silent and pensive, seemed to Calvin a crypt where feelings of superiority and independence go to die. He felt small here—he felt weak. As he boarded the elevator and considered this feebleness, his eyes glanced down toward the metal cube he carried. His finger tapped the surface of the box and caused it to slide open ever so slightly—brilliant scarlet light flooded into the room as dusk settled in beyond the glass elevator.

The feelings of smallness passed—Calvin had *remembered*.

ELEVEN

"Sir!"

"Yes, Demetria?"

"One of our investigators received a tip from the killer, not five minutes ago."

"Interesting! What did it entail?"

"Something big, sir. Shall I read it?"

"No, throw it in the furnace and burn the damn thing. Read it!"

"Yessir. It says: *Tonight, I shall cut off the head.* What might that mean?"

"...It is metaphorical, you must understand. Just as the head is lord of the body, so will the murderer's victim be someone in authority."

"Like you, sir?"

"Let's hope not."

"Will we do anything at all?"

"How many students arrived this semester to major in Academic Military?"

"About two hundred, sir."

"Ah! That will be quite enough."

"What will they do, sir? We can't just send in an *army* and pretend no one will notice!"

"You remember Statute 528.491(a), which the City Council ratified last month?"

"Not...no, sir."

"It was deliberately lengthy, of course, but one of the clauses casually mentioned that the Academy had the authority to institute martial law in the absence of an elected politician."

"And?"

"Your questions tire me, Demetria. Order the instructors to have all their students on preparatory standby. We must not be caught off guard."

I.

OUT OF THE DREGS OF A STIFF WHISKEY, MAYOR SAMUEL KAUFMANN contemplated the destiny of the City he was doomed to steer. He sat in a subdued position at his yellowed, two-person dining table, clear of everything except the bottle of spirits and the empty placemat that reminded him how alone he was. The house, as always in the midnight hour, stood like a dark shadow above him. It was too big for a single man, but municipal traditions had passed the home's deed to whoever held the office of Mayor.

A sentiment of paranoia, likely brought on by the alcohol, had taken hold in his mind. He knew the cards weren't stacked in his favor—he remembered well the outrageous ruling of the emergency hearing and the loyalties both forged and broken that day.

The Academy was against him; that was certain. In every confrontation they spun an unmatchable web of doublespeak and mystery, never releasing a definitive opinion on politics, the murders, or any affair they involved themselves into. The Academy was a dynamic power that claimed no alliance, one day your enemy, one day your friend, their goals entangled in obscurity.

The City Council was a puppet of the Academy. They were no more trustworthy than their masters.

And Paragon? Now deprived of its most incorruptible member, it stood little chance against the forces and influences that commanded the fate of the situation. Myles was an inexperienced young man, already useless before the crisis.

And Kaufmann did not know what to think of Calvin. Kaufmann had just seen him earlier that evening—on the errand of delivering their daily findings. But something had changed in his demeanor. He was no longer courteous or charming, but cold and resolute in everything he did. Melissa's passing had awoken a demon inside of him—could it supply the perseverance to solve it all? Or would it instead bring Calvin to ruin?

Kaufmann's thoughts turned to his city again. Would it resolve its troubles at the killer's first mistake? Would it slowly depopulate until every citizen was dead or in flight?

Would he live to see either outcome?

"I don't suppose you could offer me a shot, sir?"

Kaufmann's arms flew to his chair in a uncontrollable grip of terror. He was here!

"I don't believe we've met," he croaked through trembled breath.

"Isn't that the thing with public offices, Mr. Kaufmann? Everyone knows you before you know them."

"I don't recall letting you into my house."

"This sudden hostility is alarming! I thought we might be friends." Contemptuous and drawling, the stranger's voice drove an insidious, creeping fear through Kaufmann's veins.

"Friends! Okay, let's be friends. Alright? Let's take it easy now," Kaufmann whispered, and then, stammering into a spiel of banter: "Would you like a drink? Here, come over to the other end of the table, I'll grab a glass for you, you'd like that I bet, I'm sure you'd like that a lot."

"I'd like that, Mr. Kaufmann."

Kaufmann rose from his seat, amazed at the opportunity he was receiving. He extended one hand up toward the cupboard containing the glassware, and sent his other to grope around the knife block.

It was empty!

"I've taken the liberty of relieving you of those, Mr. Kaufmann," the man yawned. "I've also relieved you of a certain meat cleaver, a few frying pans...oh! and the rolling pin."

Kaufmann glanced around sadly, but he still had cards to play.

"I suppose you could throw the shot glass at me, or a good other number of things...or we could just talk. All the background, all the context, everything you wanted to know about the murders and why they occurred. If that interests you in any way, then do me a kindness and pour some whiskey before you sit down."

Kaufmann fumbled over the decision. An overwhelming tiredness gripped him—if the man had taken such precautions already, wouldn't he be prepared for any attack Kaufmann attempted? And how greatly he wished to know how the murders had all transpired! The desire supplanted his very will to survive! Conceding defeat, Kaufmann took the shot glass, poured a drink, and slid it toward the man.

"I wonder, Mr. Kaufmann, if you ever came across this concept," the man began. "If you give a child a sandcastle, and tell him that this sandcastle, which is his to command, is the greatest castle on this earth—won't he believe you? Won't he believe you, having never controlled anything before and seeing nothing greater on the horizon? And even if you yourself have no castle, are you not more influential than the child, this King of Sand who knows nothing of the world except what you've told him?"

Kaufmann paused in measured despair. "Is Comatose..." he whispered, "is Comatose *my* sandcastle?"

The man eyed him with a cold, almost pitying stare. "You are perceptive, Mr. Kaufmann. You may ask three questions of me—I will tell you what the murderer *is*. And then I must send you to sleep."

Twelve

"We followed your advice sir. The investigators arrived at his estate and found it just as you predicted. Kaufmann is comatose."

"It was only a matter of time."

"This is astounding, sir. Oh, death will come to us all!"

"No, it will not. Not if we put our foot in the door."

"Do you mean martial law, sir?"

"That's only the beginning, but we must act immediately. What time is it now?"

"6:00 AM, sir."

"By eight, I want a procession of our full strength organized and on the streets. Every able-bodied person will be assembled in the Cross to hear their new instructions."

"What of the City Council, sir? Won't they oppose martial law?"

"With our reputation, Mrs. McPherson, they will be perfectly happy to let us take the reins. Until, of course, the realization hits them that those reins will never be returned."

I.

THEY MADE NO NOISE AS THEY GLIDED—LIKE GHOSTS—ACROSS THE sprawling main road.

A caravan of sleek, white, luxury cars, dispatched from the Academy.

But this time they were followed by the steady sound of footsteps. All along Avenue Grand, like a midwinter's parade, regiments of soldiers marched in perfect unison, each unit armored in clean, ivory-tinted uniforms. Equipped with energized batons that could throw a protester's muscles into immobilizing spasms, the army was the finest crowd-control force the city had ever seen— perhaps the finest it would ever see again.

Attached to every car in the procession was a megaphone, which announced the following message to the crisp morning sky:

"MAYOR KAUFMANN IS DEAD. ALL RESIDENTS ARE HEREBY ORDERED TO EXIT THEIR HOMES AND TO GATHER AT THE CROSS FOR AN EMERGENCY ASSEMBLY."

Out of a pillow of paper and a mattress of overwhelming work, Calvin jolted awake to the noise. He was still at his desk. The deafening clamor from the procession relented for no sleeper, even one who had contributed so greatly against the danger all around them. He glanced around his dreary office as though in search of something.

"Myles?" He groaned.

Nothing. His coworker must have left earlier that evening. He stumbled to his feet, his frustration building steadily: this interruption would not permit his return to that stolen sleep! Glancing at his appearance, and finding it to be lackluster and disappointing, he settled with the proposition that every other citizen answering the call would be in a comparable state.

Calvin stepped outside and blinked in the brisk, hazy sunlight. An imperial procession of white luxury cars and armored soldiers was crawling along toward the center of town.

"MAYOR KAUFMANN IS DEAD. ALL RESIDENTS ARE HEREBY ORDERED TO EXIT THEIR HOMES AND TO GATHER AT THE CROSS FOR AN EMERGENCY ASSEMBLY."

Calvin glanced down the street, whence the endless stream of cars and soldiers seem to originate from. He saw more people on the sidewalk than he had ever seen before, all of them confused like himself. Down that direction he also saw soldiers entering the houses of the "uncooperative" citizens.

Finally, there came a section of the procession which made everything clear to Calvin. First came four phantoms with brilliant, rippling white flags attached to their sides. On these great flags was stitched the unmistakable insignia of the Academy, a bronze capital "A."

Behind these marched a tight platoon of the soldiers, each holding broad banners like those of the cars before them. As they marched along, Calvin began to suspect that another object moved within this crowd, jumping from shadow to shadow in order to remain unseen.

A sudden cessation of the platoon's movements drew his attention, and a deep, guttural growl seemed to come from somewhere within the earth itself. A vehicle, like nothing Calvin had ever seen before, then strode forth in absolute, frictionless beauty. The smoldering panther that was Morgan Powers' personal convoy had finally made itself known to the world. Between nine, sword-like shafts of metal in the grille came jets of hot flame. The long, luxurious vehicle no longer had need for concealment. Now, not merely a panther—but a great, black dragon!

And within the magnificent carriage sat Mr. Morgan Powers, his head inclined with amused intrigue, as a demigod might while traversing mortal lands. He wore a magnificent three-piece, a cream-colored, double-breasted tailcoat with vest and tie to match. From his peaked lapels shone a bronze "A" pin, indicative of his allegiance to the only government that seemed to matter now: The Academy. Calvin couldn't help himself. He stared at the procession's grand marshal in awe.

As the centerpiece of the procession rolled past Calvin, one of Powers' slow, searching glances fell on him. There was no recognition in those eyes—and why would there be? What need had Powers for acknowledgement now? Here was a man who no longer needed to trifle in the affairs of lesser men. Here was a man who was called into greatness by divinity.

"MAYOR KAUFMANN IS DEAD. ALL RESIDENTS ARE HEREBY ORDERED TO EXIT THEIR HOMES AND TO GATHER AT THE CROSS FOR AN EMERGENCY ASSEMBLY."

After the panther had passed him, after that indifferent gaze had moved on from him without ceremony, the Academy's color guard filed in behind the vehicle and continued their march. Calvin decided to keep in pace with these flag-bearing soldiers. He hadn't the faintest understanding of the Academy's new ploy—but this swift display of authority was unlike Powers' subtle stratagems. This was almost a victory march, as a chess player might in moving his rook back and forth to delay the destruction of the enemy's king.

As the head of the convoy presently reached the Cross, the procession broke into quarters and permeated into the rest of the city to awaken her sleepers. The soldiers formed tight lines around the small park which the traffic circle encompassed, and formed a barrier against the gathering crowd.

Powers, upon reaching this enclosure, disembarked from his vehicle and exchanged a few words with the technicians already preparing for the assembly. Calvin moved closer to the soldiers' perimeter as confused, drowsy citizens permitted his passage.

And at the top of that hill, he saw now, stood the ruined remains of a phone booth...

No! He would not relive these memories. Things were afoot that preyed on peace and happiness—to venture into the realm of despair would be the enemy's victory. He would not relive these memories. Not now.

The Academy had thoughtfully built a small stage on top of the crater—where that odious explosion had brought about Melissa's death. It was a touching tribute, like how one might station their shiny new car over a gravestone for lack of a parking spot.

The remainder of the procession, entering the Cross from its return voyage, led another group of confused citizens to the center of town. A technician adjusted a microphone to Powers' height. For the next few minutes, all the world held its breath in anticipation of this surprising development. Silence, like a hazy mist interspersed throughout the crowd, reigned over the whispering footsteps of the awestruck citizens.

Then Powers surveyed his subjects from the podium, and spoke.

"Citizens of Comatose. My name is Morgan Powers."

A searching gaze spanned from one end of the spectators to the other, reassuring and tranquilizing the confused crowd whose throats already lay in the firm grip of silence. At his observance tremors subsided and erratic breaths stabilized. The entire city stood in collective now, at the mercy of a man whose very whim could instill the terror of an invincible army or the serenity of a soft and comforting fireplace.

"No words can express," he continued, "the absolute terror...that has shaken the entirety of Dormido Valley. This last night, Mayor Samuel Kaufmann was taken by the inexplicable phenomena that has stricken more than thirteen citizens already."

But who in this crowd would have such knowledge? More than half of these citizens had been hiding in their holes, believing whatever they felt was true, never inspiring within themselves a desire to affirm the assumptions they made. These were the strangers who lived in the same city as other strangers, who bought the same food and wore the same clothes.

Yet of each other, of the affairs of the world and the beings that inhabited it, they knew nothing at all.

Powers went on to explain the previous deaths to this uninformed crowd. Calvin noted how the man carefully omitted any references to the terms "killed" and "murderer." The discretion was somewhat logical...but Calvin wondered at Powers' intentions.

"I spoke with the city council this morning," Powers proceeded, his compassion now transitioning into a voice of control and composure. "They, of course, are badly shaken, but action must be taken immediately. In accordance with Comatose's municipal code, I am authorized to institute martial law over the city until such political arrangements can be made. In lieu of a deputy mayor, a position that has been unfilled for many years now, the council has chosen to appoint me as the Emergency Chancellor, until an official election can be arranged."

Backed by his display of strength, both in poise and military presence, Powers' delineation of his emergency plans seemed straightforward and irreproachable. "And we shall not have to wait long, my friends. In those days we shall be free of fear. My good friends at Paragon PI are busy working on the solution to this mystery. They tell me they are very close. A matter of days, they tell me."

Powers then acknowledged Calvin's existence with a deliberate stare. The man's face spoke of respect and admiration for Calvin's contributions, but his countenance was unsettlingly false. A curious gleam had entered the man's eyes—a hint to a sudden, crippling blow: "And, if there is no such success from Paragon, then they'll be answerable to you."

Calvin blinked. His bottom lip trembled in fury.

"Damn him!" Calvin whispered, indifferent to the crowd around him. The deadline to yield a solution to the crisis had been overwhelming before this statement—now the entire city would expect Paragon's answer before the week was out.

"There are some important matters regarding the Academy's martial law that I will now be obliged to share with you," Powers continued. "These regulations will be strictly enforced by the Academy's Martial Corp, the members of which you see gathered here today. We do not understand the nature of the phenomenon that has stricken many of our citizens, but we are prepared for criminals who will seek to take advantage of this fearful time. Therefore, the assemblage of soldiers you see today are not soldiers of war, but guardians of protection. You must heed any of their orders without question, not for their benefit—but for yours."

It was a skillfully crafted simplification. In his persuasive and approachable tone, Powers had transcended the position of lecturer—he had become the conductor of a city wide orchestra, one that would obey anything from the slightest flick of the wrist to the broadest surge of the baton. Powers procured a gilded piece of paper from his jacket pocket and began to read off of it.

"There will now be a curfew over this town, which will start promptly at sundown. Guards will be patrolling the streets all night long. I would hate for them to mistake any of you for a slinking criminal." Powers voice was laced with indifference. One could never tell what he thought of the audience, but the man's dispassionate demeanor revealed to Calvin how little Powers regarded them.

"If you must leave your house, never leave it empty. I'd advise that your departures remain infrequent," Powers read. "You must never answer your door, unless it is to one of these guardians below. Each evening they will report to your door and inform you of everything that you need to know. Never accept advice or information from anyone else—they are not to be trusted."

How conclusively Powers spread the fear of one's own neighbors! He had, in under fifty words, induced a complete dependence to him and his information—no other source would suffice. Calvin glanced around at the citizens, who were readily nodding their heads at Powers' latest caution. No one felt more secure than in the intellectual embrace of a superior mind—the repetition of history over centuries of autocracy was unfolding here too! A leader who can offer safety, even at the cost of personal liberty, is a leader worth following!

"Finally, every morning starting at 8:00 AM, there will be an inspection. Every family must stand outside of their home at a procession similar to this morning's. There we shall conduct searches that will bring this affair to a swift and satisfying end. Do not be alarmed—if you have nothing to hide, you will have nothing to fear."

He paused. "There must be no one inside the house. Sick, elderly, frail? If you truly care about them, bring them out of the house."

The gilded paper carelessly slipped out of his fingers as he released it. He raised his face to look at the crowd—with the most callous, inhuman expression Calvin had ever seen.

"Clear the streets!" a husky voice barked. The line of soldiers surrounding Powers' dais made a uniform cracking sound and slowly marched forward against the crowd. Rapidly, the citizens dispersed.

Calvin ran towards his office, but something stopped him. He felt that familiar, overwhelming suspicion of another's eyes observing his movements.

Morgan Powers, from his high position atop the dais, contemplated him. Of course it was Morgan Powers. The eyes of Calvin's new enemy sat fixed upon him, watching his each and every move. They burned with an intangible flame, challenging him to escape the imminent checkmate.

Calvin turned his gaze to the forested hills above Comatose. There he might find a quiet, gravel road...and some advice, perhaps.

II

A BLAST OF BRISK, MOUNTAIN AIR BLEW INTO CALVIN'S LUNGS AND reminded him how pleasant the world could be if he took the time to enjoy it. He had escaped from the steamy sauna that was the crisis of Comatose, and in this deep and meaningful environment, Calvin aimed to regroup his senses, in order to tackle the Academy's startling new tactics.

Once again he glanced down at the city of ants, where from his standpoint all was calm and peaceful. Once again he parked his car next to the modest, unassuming gate.

451, Quiet Gravel Road. He was at the right address.

Little had changed since his last visit. He nodded amicably at the manicured lawns of the McCain Estate, thoroughly losing himself in the country aura. The Manor, still surrounded by tall rosebushes, lay before him—a window into a simpler world. One such bush, during his absence, had extended a long tendril into the main path. A traveller would have to sidestep the obstruction in order to continue. At the end of this vine a bright red rose had flowered for Calvin's pleasure. He stood a moment to admire it, but suddenly a buzz of iron wings interrupted him, and one of the gardening machines flew between him and the flower.

It was rather like an oversized hummingbird. Held aloft by graceful wings, the robot's beak was adorned with sharp blades similar to those of a garden clipper. With a brisk and utterly mechanical motion, the machine severed the flower from its bush and spirited it away.

The gesture produced in Calvin an inexplicable sadness. The scene was an odious metaphor of the real world: the generosity of nature, adulterated by mankind's greed.

But Calvin had business here. He would not dwell on this stupid flower or that stupid bird. He had business here.

At the door, Jarvis met him with that same, thin smile.

"Mr. Barker. I'm glad you've returned."

Jarvis bade him into the sitting room, where he poured out two glasses of refreshing ice water. They each took a long drink, and then Calvin began his questioning.

"Were you met this morning by soldiers from the Academy?"

Jarvis raised his eyebrows. In the background of the organized, aluminum-furnished sitting room, even this perplexed glance seemed sophisticated and intelligent.

"Soldiers? No, my friend. In fact, you were the last person to visit."

Calvin seemed taken aback. "Surely Powers knows there are citizens in this area?"

"Certainly he knows of us. Whether he *cares* what we say, think, or do, is another matter entirely. Have you news from the city?"

Calvin grimaced. "Mayor Kaufmann...he's dead. Powers responded as though he'd been hovering over the deathbed! Somehow he got a measure passed that allows him to institute martial law whenever the city finds itself without a leader."

"Kaufmann," Jarvis whispered, a tone of melancholy entering his voice. "It's a shame; he was a good friend of mine. Foolish, for trying to control an uncontrollable town, but an upright man, nonetheless."

"Everything happened too quickly. I had no time to investigate the scene of the crime because the Academy had already prepared a huge parade of cars and soldiers."

Slowly, Jarvis glanced up. "Are you quite certain, then, that he is dead?"

Calvin glanced at him, unconvinced. "Are you suggesting the Academy is to blame? Do you mean to say that they merely deposed the Mayor, sent him packing, and made him pinky-promise to keep quiet?"

Jarvis wore his typical, indecipherable mask of emotion—how similar it was to Melissa!

"I daresay that everything works in their favor," Jarvis murmured.

Calvin cast a thoughtful glance out the window. "Do you really think they're orchestrating all of this?"

"The murders?" Jarvis exclaimed. "I doubt it. But they're aware of the pattern and now they're using it."

"That's all good and well, but I can't bother myself with their gambits when there's a murderer on the loose," Calvin vented.

"I told you before to take the bigger picture into account," Jarvis reproached. "Do you still believe you can solve this affair without a comprehension of the massive changes happening within the world?"

Something inexplicable happened in Calvin—a simmering layer of tension suddenly snapped and released a savage burst of uncontrollable emotion.

"You don't understand!" he cried. A rush of blood surged into Calvin's skull—a sensation of lightheadedness and fever plagued his body and encouraged a response of animated frustration. "Melissa's death was my fault, and I need to make up for it! If I had just used my full capabilities *before* that scoundrel got so damn powerful, Melissa wouldn't have to be lying all cold and stiff in the morgue! I could have *done* something, Mr. McCain!"

Jarvis raised his eyebrows again—he had not expected to find this fierce passion at such a surface level. It was a dangerous place to keep an emotion so strong; it was akin to finding boiling water barely below the brim of the pot.

"Melissa's death," he began sternly, "was not anyone's fault but the murderer's. What I'm saying is that—"

"I understand what you're saying, and I understand how irrelevant it is to the problem at hand!" In his rage, all attempts at respect had dissolved. He stood, pacing around the room in his exasperation. "All your *talk* about politics and worldly affairs won't do a damn thing to resolve this crisis! Have you been out there, Mr. McCain? Have you any knowledge at *all* about crime save what you find in books and novels? People don't kill people to advance a political movement, they kill people for selfish, trivial things!"

Alarm crept into Jarvis's mind—this storm must be settled peacefully and immediately. "Calvin, Calvin, calm yourself, turn an ear to reason—"

"Reason?" Calvin cried. "Coming from you, the scornful little bookworm who hides away from the danger and mocks the foolish idiots who stand up for themselves? Old man, I respected you once. You think you're so pensive in this little hole of yours, but you're just as blind as them all—and just as afraid, too. I'm the one who dirties my feet to find the truth!"

Calvin turned to leave, his mind churning with feelings of anger and triumph. The latter emotion, however, was rapidly fading, as he began to realize how utterly unnecessary the outburst was, and how deeply he may have offended the man.

"Calvin!" Jarvis gasped.

No, he could not hold himself to this new, proud demeanor. Calvin turned to face the old man, the old man who had done him no wrong, the old man who had given him sage advice only to have it rejected by youthful conceit.

Jarvis's lip trembled. "I...I fear we will not see each other again. We mustn't part ways like this. Not...not like..."

Like Melissa.

"We will see each other again, Mr. McCain. I will return." Too angry to apologize and too ashamed to look upon his heartbroken old face, Calvin turned away.

"Calvin!"

No, he would not look upon that heartbroken old face. He would walk on, untouched by grace nor love nor anything else worthwhile in this world. He would walk past the ivy covered gates of 451 Quiet Gravel Road.

And he would never return.

Thirteen

"In a stabler government, Demetria, this latest step would be treason."

"It was a remarkable success, sir."

"Remarkable, you say? I find it quite understandable—I can almost picture the history books in the years to follow, outlining perfectly the stepping stones to our rise. But come now, I get too far ahead of myself. The taste of victory is a toxic wine!"

"Always cautious to the end, you are. Might I suggest an hour of actual respite?"

"The moment I begin to relent is the moment my opponent strikes hardest. And we are drawn more taut than ever before. Should the murderer strike before we can cover the situation, our public statements will be invalidated by our lack of caution. And should Paragon unveil the identity of the threat, the fulcrum of our influence will be stripped from us. No Demetria, we cannot rest!"

"Forgive my criticism, sir, but if we had removed Paragon much earlier, they would not be a thorn in our side now."

"You are quite right, Demetria, but it cannot be helped. From what I gather, Paragon is in a *tight* financial situation."

"They were privately engaged by Kaufmann? Or by the City?"

"It was a private arrangement. It will make Pruitt's job much easier when he goes in to suspend their funding, despite Kaufmann's last will and testament, which incidentally fell into our possession. I still remain dumbfounded that Kaufmann would actually bequeath a dividend to continue Paragon's investigation posthumously!"

"It *is* astonishing, sir. If I may..."

"Always you accuse *me* of caution! It's *you* who can never seem to muster the courage to utter an opinion contrary to mine! Say what you will."

"You are generous, sir. I should like to point out my distaste in relying on Pruitt's methods when a more direct approach remains untrodden. Surely there is a faster way to dissolve this opponent? You yourself mentioned how you had been 'sowing the seeds of discord.' How is your garden growing?"

"That's actually a point I wanted to raise with you. I've spoken with young Master Goodrich already, but am unsure what he thinks of me. Perhaps you can convince him of the futility of his work."

"Consider it done."

I.

MYLES, ALONE IN THE OFFICE AS USUAL, WAS PREOCCUPIED TO THE highest extent his brain could provision the capacity for. He had made several phone calls in the last half hour, and was engaged in the studying of complicated reports. A half-eaten bagel had been thoughtlessly cast aside in the pressure of work.

During this time, he did not put a single thought toward the case. It had the rather unfortunate effect of giving him a headache. But tax season was coming soon. "After all," he murmured amicably, "one mustn't fall behind on important deadlines."

A ringing came from somewhere nearby. The phone! Excellent. Mr. Pruitt from Pruitt & Sons Monetary Affairs was finally returning his call from last night.

"Yes, this is Chief Inspector Myles Goodrich." Another lie, although arguably true at this point. What with Calvin running in and out of the office and never casting a glance at the rent, Myles had to take initiative. Calvin was just too negligent to run the business!

"Have you considered my proposal from yesterday?" Mr. Pruitt asked. "I think you'll find it beneficial in the end."

Myles needed to be clever—this was *professional* business. "Yes, Mr. Pruitt, but I could not overcome the doubts that I likewise expressed," Myles replied, spouting off a verbose rebuttal. "Will the potential gain offset your firm's expenses? You expect to be paid...how much again?"

"Oh, I believe that will be a trivial matter, Mr. Goodrich. You see, the Emergency Chancellor put in a few good words at his address this morning, and I think it highly likely your revenue will skyrocket at the conclusion of this case, a case which, for a man of your intelligence, can hardly remain unsolved for long."

Flattered, Myles grinned, and made sure to make absolutely no comment on the actual progress of the case. He'd thank Calvin later.

"So, the expenses...?"

"Let's propose, for the moment, that our consultant begins at $10,000 a month—a fair starting salary on our part, and a very safe investment on yours. The Kaufmann Estate is paying you, as I recall from your free consultation, $15,000 from a monthly dividend. You may have to tighten your belt for a week or two, but hear me out—upon closing your current investigation, the positive effect on your public relations will allow you to double, nay, even triple your asking price. Doesn't that sound favorable?"

It...it did. "But...well, won't you raise your prices consistent with our growth?"

The reply was warm and sincere. "Of course not! Our consultants will remain at the starting salary until you've reached a financial position that's stable enough to make a new venture."

Myles was *almost* convinced.

"Did I mention," the man added wryly, "the perks?"

"Perks?"

"Custom mailing labels. Monogrammed cotton envelopes. Ball-point pens with PARAGON PRIVATE INVESTIGATIONS printed on the side. All the stylings of a professional entity."

Myles's eyes widened. "Show me what to do!"

This semblance of a strategic partnership continued through the night as Myles blithely turned over Paragon's billing information to the fraudulent consulting firm and laid out the particulars with Mr. Pruitt—Secretary of Finance and Internal Affairs at the Academy. When all had finished, he heartily ripped off a chunk of bagel with his teeth, leaned back in his chair, and sighed with content.

"Mr. Goodrich."

Myles yelped in surprise. The voice was feminine—someone had infiltrated his office unseen. His gaze immediately flew to the source of the startling phrase, where he found Ms. Demetria McPherson from the Academy standing near his desk.

"Oh. It's you," Myles muttered, through a mouthful of bagel.

"Mr. Goodrich, I'm speaking on behalf of Emergency Chancellor Powers—"

"Of course you are."

Ms. McPherson did not seem surprised by his disrespectful interruptions. In fact, she seemed prepared for such remarks. With an almost covert demeanor, she said: "And...of my own accord."

Myles glanced up at her with mild surprise. People from the Academy never spoke for themselves!

"Fine. What do you want to tell me?"

"E.C. Powers wanted to inform you that Paragon has very little time remaining to solve the case. In three days, he plans to suspend your investigation."

This was ridiculous. It was bad enough that Powers kept giving himself fancy titles—but now he had to go and threaten everyone else!

"What's this?" Myles voiced aloud. "Powers can't play nice? Doesn't he have enough toys without having to steal from the other children on the block? We're employed by Kaufmann, and we won't be leaving the case until he tells us to!"

Ms. McPherson gave him a very brief, sideways glance of confusion. "Mr. Goodrich...did you not hear the news? Mayor

Kaufmann is comatose, practically dead. He has been so for more than twenty-four hours, in fact."

Myles blinked. Of course he knew that. But...if Kaufmann was no longer paying them...

"Have you reached the conclusion I speak of, Mr. Goodrich? Kaufmann's accounts have been posthumously frozen. From a business standpoint, you must realize that there is no real reward."

Myles froze—hopefully he could cancel the bill with the consulting firm *before* they drained all of Paragon's remaining funds.

"And...I'm speaking strictly off record, Mr. Goodrich, but..." she paused, hesitant. To Myles, at least, it was believable. "You are faced with a choice, as the business leader of your company. If you do manage to solve the case, you will of course become one of the most prestigious detective firms in the area. You'll be able to place satellite firms in Anesthesia and the other great cities. But if you fail..."

Myles reflected on that possibility. He reflected on a more realistic version of Paragon, a version that had bit off more than it could chew and sank into notoriety forever...

"Mr. Goodrich, you can consider this case your last, if you do not succeed. People are talking about you. They're saying that you're the Hercule Poirot of this generation. Global success and brilliant fame could be in your future! But there is a lot on the line."

Myles raised a hand up to his head and contemplated the scenarios. There *was* a lot on the line. Say they failed: Even the missing cat cases would go to another firm! Everyone would remember Paragon as the firm that couldn't solve the Comatose Case.

Ms. McPherson continued softly: "And your...coworker? Calvin Barker? Where has he been?"

Myles face contorted into something akin to disgust. "He's been working. I...I don't know where he's been."

"You must, of course, consider that he's taken Melissa's death rather poorly. But, when all comes to light, you also must decide when you believe he's abandoned you. And if he truly has abandoned you...what will come of the case? I...I speak very out of turn, Mr. Goodrich, but: if all of the Academy's detectives have been unsuccessful thus far...how is Paragon going to compete with only one man?"

Myles frowned.

Ms. McPherson, with a smirk, finished it out: "How would it feel, having all of Comatose blame Paragon's demise...on you?"

Myles was scared now. Scared of the truth.

The skeletal woman withdrew a shiny business card from a handbag of sharp, snow-white leather. She handed it to him and waited as he briefly read the contact information.

"The Academy has ways of making people disappear. And a man with your kind of talents has a place in our Forensics Department. You would thrive there, Mr. Goodrich. There are so many opportunities waiting for you. Paragon—the entire 'Private Eye' concept—it's a childish and romantic idea. Why be a copper cog when the clockwork's gold?"

"I'll consider your proposal," Myles heard himself say.

"I hope you will."

She smiled at him primly, and then turned around and exited the office. Seconds later, a white phantom crept away from the office—and Myles was alone once more.

But now, for the first time, he felt alone.

FOURTEEN

"Your talk with Master Goodrich was most impressive, Ms. McPherson!"

"Thank you, sir."

"I mean it! These are the small stones which will start the avalanche."

"I thought you had expressed your distaste for clichés, Mr. Powers."

"Very well. I'll cut the gratitude and you'll cut the snide remarks."

"Fine with me, sir."

"Ah—what time is it now?"

"A few minutes to midnight."

"And Master Goodrich has already expressed his interest in...joining us?"

"Readily. Once Mr. Pruitt explained the irreversible nature of the consulting fee, Myles put all of Paragon's accounts under Calvin Barker's name. Mr. Goodrich says he'll be here early tomorrow morning."

"Then I must congratulate Mr. Pruitt's efforts in junction with yours. We seem to have gained $10,000 through the affair."

"An agreeable bonus, to be sure—will it be tracked back to us?"

"Isn't that the beauty of it all, Ms. McPherson? No one is looking. With Myles taken care of for now, we are left with Calvin. Unfortunately, he cannot be bought. We'll have to hasten this part of The Project."

"What will be done tonight?"

"I'll send someone to warn every councilor to lock their doors."

"Will that help?"

"Of course not."

I.

INSPECTION.

Not one house had been left occupied by the citizens of Comatose. They had listened well; they had taken a tentative step away from the dirty floor of ignorance and toward the waiting arms of their new parents, the Academy.

The streets filled themselves with startling aspects of a fascist parade—in every direction, all that could be seen were colors of pearl and bronze. On the pennants of the Academy, on the gleaming bodies of the silent phantoms or the shining armor of the silent peacekeepers, the glory of the Academy strode forward, unchallenged and utterly dominant. The obsidian panther crept in pace with the crux of the procession, its presence sending a shudder through the waiting crowd. In the chill of the morning it was a furnace—in the brilliance of the sun it was a spot of midnight.

The color guard again marched around the sleek, deadly vehicle, their flags an ostentatious reproach to the citizens. With exaggerated movements, the banners danced around like the flags of a self-proclaimed empire.

Calvin's residence stood between the Academy's campus and his office, and was only a block away from the latter. He stood outside of his abode, like any good citizen might, and scrutinized the soldiers who briskly searched his house.

The radiant center of the parade had entered Calvin's view, but he immediately suspected something would be different today. Two soldiers were approaching him, their eyes alight in the thrill of a special assignment.

"Keep walking forward, Mr. Barker," the men ordered. Calvin complied, turning his back to them and following the flow of the procession. The lead vehicle slowed so that Calvin could join Powers for whatever purpose he had been procured. The wall of flag bearers parted with dexterous uniformity, and to Calvin's astonishment, so did the particles of the panther's door.

A moment's hesitation granted him the liberty to examine the expansive, roofless interior of the vehicle. The chairs, like locomotives on a train track, could move along a smooth metal rail to multiple position within the vehicle. Powers turned the wheel over to Ms. McPherson, and then maneuvered his seat to face Calvin, who clambered into the panther and took a chair of his own.

Powers' voice, this time, was sincere and grim: "Have you found our man?"

Calvin regarded his rival coldly; he contemplated the viable responses and their outcomes. While Calvin labored the hours away searching for an explanation to their crisis, this man marched his toy army around the city each morning, like a child! Here was a man, an enemy, who couldn't care less about the results of Calvin's discovery.

"What's it to you?" Calvin hissed.

Powers regarded him with an air of discontent. "I've been troubled lately, Mr. Barker, with your increasingly hostile attitude— it has become detrimental to our cooperation. The identity of this villain *must* be unveiled. You see, the murderer has struck again— last night."

Calvin paused, interested—albeit in a rather displeased fashion. He always hated how the Academy managed to learn about murders before he did.

But Calvin's mind, in Powers eyes, was encased in a transparent skull—every thought could be easily perceived. "Of course, it wasn't our detectives who discovered the murders. It was, in fact, myself."

"Oh? Do tell." Calvin muttered.

Powers ignored this sarcasm. "There was to be a meeting of the emergency committee and the city council this morning, only...no one showed up." The man eyed him obliquely. "By this time I'm sure that you, of all people, have learned to fear the worst."

Calvin looked at the man's now closed mouth and knew the next word behind it: *Melissa.* Ten thousand curses passed through his mind, terrible words that would bring a weaker man to his knees. Yet no feeling of hatred, no force of loathing, not even the dregs scraped from the blackest of hearts could ever inflict suffering on Morgan Powers.

Calvin retreated from these dark thoughts. "The city councilors? All of them...are dead?"

"Indeed. Thirteen councilors, dead in their homes. I must stress that five of them were former Academy employees."

Calvin made a comical, clown-like frown. The distinction made no difference to him.

Powers turned around again and was silent. Presently the sleek, black vehicle had reached the Cross. Ms. McPherson stopped the vehicle, and the exterior contorted until an opening had been made in both sides of the car.

"This is where I leave you, Mr. Barker," Powers murmured.

Calvin disembarked and absentmindedly watched white-armored soldiers form a perimeter around the traffic circle. As he made his way to the edge of this human wall, Mr. Powers stood and called to him, having apparently contemplated one last question to ask.

"Mr. Barker? You are quite sure that you have no leads, whatsoever?"

Calvin turned around. Would he tell the man that Melissa had regarded this chief of the Academy as their greatest threat?

Ha. Of course not.

"We have no strong leads at this time."

Powers returned a compassionate glance. "I see. Fear not, Mr. Barker. With a few reformations on our partnership, I believe we will be able to form a stronger union to defeat this foe."

Calvin nodded. One of the peacekeepers pulled him by the shoulder, removing him from the inner circle and expelling him beyond the perimeter into the waiting crowd—where he belonged.

By the time Calvin had regained his bearings, Powers had reached the stage. The fanfare had increased since the previous meeting with the addition of oddly permanent-looking flagpoles on either side of the dais. A rich, powerful voice suddenly began to speak: "People of the honorable City of Comatose, please stand and remove your hats in respect of Municipal Chancellor Morgan Powers!"

This was done, somewhat begrudgingly. Calvin blinked. He could have sworn that Powers had been presented as the Emergency Chancellor not two days ago.

But when Powers had taken his place at the podium, the feelings of resentment within the crowd passed. It was the appearance of a comforting father; now everything would be made right. Notwithstanding Powers' control over the crowd, Calvin felt more uneasy than ever.

"Friends. I am grieved to bring even more troubling news to you. The members of the city council have been simultaneously stricken by this deadly phenomenon."

There was little alarm. The morning was still brisk; the audience was shivering. Surely these comforts were more immediate concerns. Fewer interruptions, would, no doubt, end the speech faster.

"We must let our resolve be united, my friends. For if there is dissension among us, we will fall prey to anarchy—and nothing will be brought to fruition save death. Shall we work together for this common good?"

An unspoken yet mutual, synchronous response. *Yes, Mr. Chancellor, whatever you say!*

"Alas, we have more disappointing news. I regrettably must announce that our foremost investigative partner, Paragon PI, has come across a dead end in their search."

Calvin froze. Now, like a match struck amidst the shadows, he realized what "reformations" Morgan Powers intended to establish. Calvin could do nothing but watch as his enemy ripped apart his reputation like a book, burning each page one by one.

"The new Municipal Investigation Service discovered their empty bank account and realized that they no longer have the funds to continue operating. This morning, in my discussion with Paragon's primary investigator, I was told they had 'no strong leads at this time.' Will you join me in thanking our associates despite this insurmountable roadblock they have reached?"

Light applause arose. Calvin hated every second of it.

"Though their efforts were indeed commendable, I regrettably will be dismissing Paragon from the case and appropriating the evidence they have so far collected to our existing investigation. The unification of our joint discoveries will ensure a swifter conclusion to this crisis."

Calvin was pushing his way back through the crowd. He had to find Myles. The crowd, like specters of another world, let him pass.

"Some pleasing news at last, my friends. The M.I.S., which is run chiefly through the Academy's Forensic Department, has developed some alarming clues that could point us toward..."

Powers' voice slowly faded as Calvin ran towards his workplace. The door opened. The office was dark.

In the silent building, he searched for signs of occupancy. Why would Myles be here, all alone? He would most likely be somewhere in that ghostly crowd, hanging on to every word that left Powers' mouth, as if it were scripture.

Calvin called his name anyway.

"Myles! They shut us out. We're finished."

The empty room did not respond—not directly. Calvin was discovering that the response had been made many hours before he had entered this morning. Something about the room was notably different than when he had last entered.

He surveyed the office. Having already understood Myles' absence, he would have to search for other explanations. Melissa's desk was untouched; nothing to find there. His own desk seemed to be filled with more papers than before—what were these?

Bank receipts, tax forms...the bill for a consulting firm?

"What are these?" Calvin murmured. "They're all under *my* name."

He paused. His eyes opened wider. And then he raced to the inner office, where Myles usually worked.

Empty! All of his coworker's belongings were gone! The desk was a dark, flat surface, devoid of stain and dust altogether. A small piece of paper had been left in the center of the worktable.

Calvin, his hands shaking, lifted the note from the desk and read:

Personally hired by McPherson of the Academy's Forensics Dept. Put the accounts and stuff under your name. Good luck with the company.

There was no signature, not even a memory of the man who had once worked in this now empty room. Calvin beat the desk with his fist, and the pain was but a distant throb to his troubled mind. He beat it again and again, and then shook the note violently as if its message could somehow be erased or rearranged into one more favorable.

Personally hired by McPherson of the Academy's Forensics Dept. Put the accounts and stuff under your name. Good luck with the company.

"No." A whisper. "This is a joke, it's fake, it's a goddamn fake!" Calvin cried. "Myles!"

There was no Myles. There had never been a Myles, there had only been a self-interested man who offered snide remarks about serious issues, a treacherous man who was one moment there and the next moment gone.

Yes, Myles was gone.

And with him, the future of Paragon had departed as well.

Calvin collapsed into the chair by Myles' desk, still clutching the note that had destroyed the business forever. He was entirely alone.

"It's over," he murmured. "It's finished. We're through. The murderer has won."

His funds would run out in days, his business would never see a patron again, his house would foreclose and his neighbors turn against him. The tower of prestige he stood upon was crumbling beneath his very feet! A faceless career of starvation and bitterness awaited him now, while a new society of bronze and pearl rose above the darkness of the world. Without another glance back, without another sympathetic thought, they would leave him behind.

His life, or what he knew of his life, had ended. The curtain was descending on whoever Calvin Barker used to be, the lights were down, the mikes were off, the actor who had played him so perfectly was startled, at a loss! With a soft thud, the curtain hit the stage, and the controlled, composed Calvin Barker was no more.

A flutter of energy rose in his chest, a burst of despair consumed him! overwhelmed him! terrified him! Where was he? Who was this trembling man? He screamed! A loud, thunderous cry of desperation resounded around the empty office, and the man collapsed to the floor in anguished tremors. He paused for air, screamed again, now interspersed with violent gasps and choked with sobs.

"Gone, it's gone, lost lost lost!" Hoarse vocals were finally channeled into speech. "I'm a dead man, I'm a corpse! I'm *nothing!*"

Now forsaken, Calvin glanced about his wasteland. He remembered the note. It had been carelessly dropped in his moment of despair, and *still* it had not changed.

Personally hired by McPherson of the Academy's Forensics Dept. Put the accounts and stuff under your name. Good luck with the company.

But he experienced a deeper comprehension upon this third read. Myles, at first, had only abandoned him. But...*the Academy*? Had he somehow found a place in the bright society that had already cast Calvin out?

"Personally hired? Myles?"

He blinked. Calvin suddenly found himself standing, and very confused. Myles, as in...*Myles*? The useless, complacent, starry-eyed fool who had somehow found Melissa's favor as an intern and rose to a position of no significance whatsoever? *That* Myles?

"But...he was useless." Calvin whispered, his denial fading into a sentiment of passionate hatred. "Myles was *useless!* He never did the work, never, *never!*" He slammed his fist on the table in fury. "He doesn't deserve this recognition! *I* am the hero, *I* am the reason he ever amounted to *anything!*" With a monstrous roar, Calvin surrendered his muscles to the mechanical motions of total fury. He ran into the main atrium, found one of the guest chairs, and threw it across the room.

With a crash, the chair ripped through the contents of Melissa's desk, decimating the sacred place. The shrine of inspiration.

Calvin cried out and fell to the floor. All of his friends were gone at last. Myles, like Judas, had damned him to this fate. Everything had been taken from him! Melissa, dead! Jarvis, unreachable. And Myles...

It always came back to Myles.

"He has betrayed me..." Calvin moaned. The empty room chuckled in silence; it watched his writhing motions in amusement. Calvin scratched at the hardwood and tried to bury himself within it, but the floor offered no sanctuary from the voices pounding into his head.

Will you let this stand, Calvin? Will you allow this bumbling fool to get away with your future?

"No," he whispered. "I won't let this stand."

You're too late, Calvin. You can't save yourself, in the end.

"I can't save myself in the end," he agreed. "I have nothing left to lose."

He looked up in furious resolution. "I have nothing left to lose. I have *nothing left to lose!*"

He leaped from his sprawled position on the ground and screamed toward the buildings of the Academy. "You thought you could stab me in the back, Myles!? You thought you could walk away from this *disaster* you've caused and not feel one damned consequence of your mistakes? You were wrong, Myles Goodrich! I'm your consequence!"

His breath turned to staccato intakes and exhalations, his damp hair flew into his now bloodshot eyes. An inhuman growl, like that of a dog, suddenly left his lips:

"I'll kill that traitor."

His eyebrows raised in alarm—but the idea was appealing. He tried it again!

"I'll kill that traitor!"

Something hanging above the door caught his attention—it was the picture frame—and he remembered well what stood within it. He whimpered at the sight. It was the photo from the picnic, that long-dead memory of laughter and contentment. There, in that picture frame, lay three innocent smiles: Calvin's, Myles's, and Melissa's.

He moaned to himself as he stepped toward the photo.

"I'm not myself, I'm not myself..." he took the frame into his hands and sobbed again. "I'm not myself, I'm not myself—"

He looked at the smile of Myles Goodrich, and suddenly Calvin knew that every evil thing that had happened to him was *this man's fault*.

There came a roar of rage, and the picture frame was thrown to the ground with an explosive shatter. "I'm not myself!" he screamed, but now with a confident resolution that he no longer wanted to be. "Myles must die! And if the damned murderer can't do his job, I'll do it for him!"

Calvin whirled around the room. He couldn't just *kill* someone! He would be caught!

And then, The Thought came to him. The obvious, perfectly arranged solution! His voice became a desolate whisper.

"But...the poison..."

He raced back to Melissa's desk and glanced up at the air vent above the worktable. He glanced at the chair he had thrown in his anger. Then, with a final utterance of hatred, he swept the desk clean with the back of his hand. Everything that once was sacred fell to the floor with a tremendous crash. Every stone had been overturned.

Calvin leapt onto the now clean desk and pried open the vent. Then, gingerly, he lifted the only thing that still mattered to him—the dark metallic cube that contained the unspeakable beauty.

Crouching, his hands shaking, he caused the box to open. Once again, the lustrous red light filled the room with a powerful, all-consuming presence. He placed his fingers around the globe and brought the impossible, all-defying sphere to meet his wondrous eyes.

His heart pounded. A war was afoot!—and he would win! His mind sank even further into lunacy as his fingers clutched the pulsating glass sphere. His heartbeat began to match the throbbing of the globe.

And finally, with the absolute power of the sphere to compel him, he willingly took the final step off the shores of sanity. "I'll kill that traitor. And the murderer, who killed my friends and tore *everything* from me—will bear the death of Myles on my behalf."

Across the empty streets and empty world Calvin glared. The image of the traitor burned within his waking eyes—the blood of twisted justice flowed within his throbbing veins.

Something had broken in Calvin's mind.

And there was no one who cared enough to fix it.

FIFTEEN

"Done. Paragon is closed off from all our online records."

"Thank you, Demetria. The game of Chess is nigh complete. Their pieces—their allies—have withered away. Only their king remains now."

"A curious metaphor sir. You have every right to straight out declare, 'Victory!'"

"The king, although unable to move far, still can strike. One mistake, Ms. McPherson, one step too close to the enemy, and our 'victory' will come to naught."

"To the bitter end, then."

"You see, Ms. McPherson, the final problem lies in the fact that the murderer still has not been caught. Many citizens will agree that we, the Academy, have benefitted inappropriately from these circumstances. An investigation against us would be most undesirable."

"They will find nothing."

"Nothing concerning this incident. But there are other things that I would rather keep unseen."

"So—"

"The plan is already afoot, but very delicate. You'll notice a key piece of evidence that I left in Paragon's possession."

"What? Wait...Sir! How could you? That's one of our most valuable assets!"

"I know. But it needs to be tested, and the results could prove extremely worthwhile in the end. So, Demetria, I outline a simple cause and effect relationship between two imminent events. The first: Myles must not be granted sanctuary here. He must return

to his own home this evening, just for one
night."
"Very well sir. And the effect?"
"The murderer, within twelve hours, shall
be caught."

I.

MYLES WAS LIKING HIS NEW OFFICE. THE ROOM, AN EXPANSIVE, 400
square-foot studio, was a showcase of the Academy's most
revolutionary, *avant-garde* ideas. The room was absent of furniture
entirely, save for some contemporary couches along the walls and a
low-to-the-ground study chair where Myles sat. In the exact center
of the room there stood a metal rod, tall as an average man. Atop
this rod was a glass sphere, casting brilliant lumens across the
studio as it shrouded the entire room in a panoramic computer
interface.

Myles finally understood the sciences of nanotechnology—
one of the Academy's most impressive developments. Similar to the
physics of Morgan Powers' car, his room was filled with airborne,
molecular-sized sensors. The glass sphere, which projected the
screen and kept track of the position of his projects, also received
information from the nano-receptors—sensors which picked up on
the smallest traces of the oils found on a human finger...

The responsiveness of this device was unbelievable—all of
this was unbelievable. With a single, spoken word, Myles ordered
the frosted glass curtains to recede, allowing him to enjoy the
stunning view from his office in the Tower.

The City of Comatose was dim that night. He saw that even
now half of the houses and buildings were dark—never to be lit
again. A long stream of cars was slowly climbing the hillside, to get
away, away, away! They would go to the Cities, the strange, orderly
societies that were doing away with currency and the human
workforce in an attempt to achieve a world that would run itself.
Their ambition? To create a system that would handle its own
affairs and allow the common man, stripped of his social
responsibilities, having no greater purpose, to curl up and die.

"And where will you go?" he asked of the pilgrims, the corners of his lips pulled upward in a smug chuckle. "The world doesn't have a place for you anymore!"

He, like these hopeless travelers, had just recently escaped from his own hell—but the Academy was something else entirely. How much had Myles learned, in but one day of working...how suddenly had circumstances thrust him into a position of reverence. How swiftly had he become a decisive player in the future of the world!

10:00. Might as well head out.

He turned away from the floor-to-ceiling window and placed his hand lightly on the glass sphere. Like a myriad of dissipating genies, the projects swarmed inward until all the sphere's light had extinguished. Myles spent only a moment in darkness. The orb reignited in white brilliance, cruel unsentimental fluorescent light. As he exited the room, the orb began to dim in pace with the swiveling door. The door closed—the light turned itself off.

Humming to himself, Myles walked down the bright hallway to the glass elevator. Out of the corner of his eye, another coworker exited a room behind him. Myles's cheerful tune drew quiet as he decided what to do.

He drew no concrete conclusions, but felt his pace quicken as the elevator came near. Too late now. Once inside, he repetitively tapped the CLOSE DOORS button to secure the stranger's fate. Alone, with only the darkling city to observe his actions, he spoke: "Employee Dorms, please."

The elevator responded. "Sincerest Apologies—*Myles Goodrich*—you do not have access to that floor."

Myles blinked. "That had been part of the arrangement..."

His hasty escape had been foiled by the elevator! Deprived of an executable order, the lift reopened its doors to admit that coworker he had trivialized. Only...

That coworker was Ms. McPherson.

His boss.

Myles cursed himself and prepared a tactful excuse—he was excellent at these. But McPherson beat him to speech.

"Having trouble with the lift controls, Myles?" she asked, sounding slightly rehearsed.

"Why yes—the elevator won't let me get to the dormitories."

She looked at him vaguely. "Oh. My sincerest apologies, Myles." Her phrasing reminded him of the elevator, monotone and unsentimental. "Mr. Powers was unable to secure a vacancy this afternoon; some more troubling matters arose that he had to deal with."

"When will—"

"Tomorrow, Mr. Goodrich, I can assure *that* much. Surely you still own a home."

Yes, no one could sell a house that fast. But...every second he spent away from this splendor seemed a second wasted—every memory of his old life, by comparison, seemed dim and squalid. With no words to say, Myles substituted a nod for the reply.

McPherson did not wait for his response. Her task, as it was, had been completed. "Ah...Commercial Department," she announced.

The elevator descended exactly one floor down and expressed a cordial farewell message to the outbound passenger. The doors opened, and Myles' employer stepped out briskly.

"Goodbye, Myles," she said loftily.

The doors closed. "Ground Floor," Myles murmured.

"A pleasure to serve you—*valued guest*. At the Academy, we strive to offer exemplary customer service," the elevator chirped as it continued its descent.

Myles found his thoughts drifting beyond the present situation, not even hearing whatever the computerized elevator spoke to him. He wondered why McPherson had made such an effort to be on the elevator at the exact time as him. He wondered why she had traversed the entire hallway when there had been an elevator on the other side of the building. He wondered why she had been so anxious to get off at the very next floor, on which she clearly had no business.

The elevator stopped. The voice wished him a good night and bade him to return soon.

Myles walked through an empty, dimly-lit reception office and then past palatial three-story doors. The brisk, evening air welcomed him into the night, inviting him to take a few tentative steps away from the majesty of the Academy. He glanced up at the huge, triangular statues which stood around the campus like shards of a god's smashed champagne glass.

Though a member of their ranks, he felt unwelcome. He felt like a new Catholic in an ominous cathedral, nervously eyeing the stained glass portraits of the saints and angels, who with icy glances seemed to accuse him of his inability to reach such commendable holiness.

Myles shivered in the cold, and in The Cold. He robed himself in the façade of contentment and complacency, but it offered no comfort. From nothingness he wove his blanket; to nothingness it would return. Did he truly consider himself a member of the Academy?

"I am among them, yet not *one* of them," he thought.

Myles walked down the intricately paved driveway, having no car to drive. His only vehicle had been the company car, which now belonged to Paragon and its owner—

But he would not think of Paragon. And he would not think of its owner.

And so he walked, in darkness, his footsteps in pace with the growing Darkness of Comatose. He took a step onto Avenue Grande, where the cars followed each other out of the town and into mystery once more. Tonight, as citizens finally informed of their fate began to act, an improvised exodus would begin—and carry on throughout the night until Comatose truly became like its name.

The streetlights provided the sole source of luminosity for Myles's weary trek home. They too had begun to dim, and though vastly different from the cold, fluorescents of the Academy, they were callous all the same. For theirs was an ancient, unwelcoming light, a light which drained the world of saturation and stained the streets in black and red.

In his home, at least, he would find the warm incandescents which he knew and loved. In his home he would find security. He walked past a dark alley, where he noted the prowlers slowly living out the rest of their lives—in a world that moved too quickly for them.

A window shattered. But Myles did not stop. He would not be consumed in the ancient darkness—he had been given a role in the bright theatre of the future!

Finally, he arrived at Calle del Durmiente. His residence was at the end of the street, past empty houses and long patches of darkness. His pace quickened in view of the homestretch, but a burst of hesitance, vague and inexplicable, kept him wary.

At last his house awaited! He opened the door and stepped in, fully expecting a warm room filled with warm light.

He found neither.

The room was cold, the same temperature as the outside. Myles considered the light switch and decided against it with deft surety. These lights would show something he did not wish to see. How conflicted it all was! The Academy, with their cold, harsh lights, the streets, with their distant, unwelcoming lights, and now his house, with lights that could only reveal shameful truths, painful truths.

So he remained in darkness.

A draft of air agitated the stillness of the room. Something had been left open. He progressed slowly through the dark house, careful to disturb nothing. He found the window in the back of his kitchen, and an icy breath met him from a mouth of crystal teeth.

It was shattered!

Myles remembered the sound he had heard in the alleyway, the window smashing. He felt sick to his stomach. *He was not alone in the house...*

The room exploded in luminescence. The Other had activated the light.

Frozen in place, Myles' first sight was the window—blood dribbled around the mess in erratic splatters. The intruder had entered with an insurmountable determination that would yield to no injury. Slowly, Myles turned around to face this resolute visitor.

"Calvin!" he cried.

MATTHEW ROBERTS | 103

The stranger grinned. This could not possibly be Calvin. But it was! His hair was damp and unkempt; his hands were covered in his own blood. And his eyes, those terrible orbs! They seemed to glow with a brilliance of their own—alight with insanity, radiant with ferocity, yet also simmering with a gruesome, desperate desire.

"Myles," he rasped, his voice edged in harrowing accusation, "you abandoned me."

Myles looked at his former friend. Something was *wrong*, something was awry, this was not the Calvin he knew from before! "Calvin," he whispered. He kept his words slow, tender. "Your hands are covered in blood, let me help—"

"*No!*" Calvin hissed.

Myles unconsciously stepped backwards.

"Let's have some tea, Myles. Put the kettle on. We'll talk."

"Your hands—"

"My hands are fine!" Calvin cried. "Sit down!"

"The tea—"

"Sit down!"

Myles, very worried now, put the kettle on and sat down at the kitchen table. Calvin sat himself across from Myles.

"Why have you done this to me, Myles? Why?"

Myles swallowed. "Left you? I put everything in your name; you are the sole owner of Paragon! What have I done to you?"

"*Done* to me! Damn you, Myles, you've left me to die!" Calvin cried.

"No, Calvin, no, no...that's not what I did..."

"Maybe you weren't there at inspection this morning," Calvin hissed. "Morgan Powers barred Paragon from the case! Imagine that, Myles." Calvin stood, and began to pace around the the table. Myles, though frightened out of his mind, did not allow himself to move. He stared straight ahead, beyond the walls of the world, and Calvin spoke to him:

"Imagine, for a minute, that you're me. Let's go back to Melissa's death. Everything was fine up until then, wasn't it? Now, you are me, remember. You tell your trustworthy coworker to handle a frightfully easy council meeting while you handle the more troubling matter of informing a father of his daughter's death.

"You're weary and heartbroken when you return," Calvin continued, "so you're really, really, looking forward to some good news. But then you learn that your coworker, against all odds, has failed you. How would that make you feel, Myles?"

Myles was silent. Calvin had posed the question rhetorically.

"And now let's imagine that you, still playacting Calvin, continue to investigate. Things are getting tough, Myles! Bam! Snap! Kaufmann's dead! Pressure, Myles! The room's getting stuffy! Powers is subtly hinting to the masses that *Paragon* is solely responsible to save the day, that *Paragon* is liable for your damages, your dead loved ones, your goddamn everything! How do you feel, Myles? Do you feel alone? Do you feel like you need some assistance? Moral support?"

Myles felt a hot tear strike his cheek.

"So you surmise: 'Surely my coworker will provide all of these things.' But you're having trouble finding him. Every two hours! You step into the office and call his name, but no answer! He's always out doing something. You try calling his phone, that'll work, right? He answers and says he's very busy on a very important lead. But you check his desk and there's nothing there at all. Well—nothing save *tax forms* and *bank receipts*.

"You start to wonder, Myles! You think to yourself, as the sun sets on another day of uselessness, 'Will the cycle ever end? Am I the sole source of progress—am I the reason we stay afloat?'"

Calvin paused. "And you ask the darker questions, too. 'Is there a leech in the business? Is there another investigator in this office, or just a sizable paycheck that gets mailed out for the half hour he comes in?'"

Myles buried his face in his hands. But Calvin wasn't done yet.

"You wonder, *god* you wonder! And meanwhile, Myles, things are still happening on the outside! Bam! Snap! Pressure increasing again! In fact, the pressure gets to be too much for the coworker. He decides to leave. Oh! What a thoughtful young fellow! This coworker of yours leaves the unfinished affairs to your already full plate, and best of all, he's done everything wrong. He's blown half the emergency savings on a consulting firm—as if they were the damned gods of money, as if a snap of their fingers would resurrect a withering business! Bam! Snap! The balloon finally pops. Powers takes the needle and terminates your only source of income."

Calvin stopped pacing. "And what a state has that coworker left your business in."

Myles was sobbing. He felt Calvin's hatred and cringed beneath it. The kettle was screaming.

"Now, I suppose we're done imagining, Myles. I suppose you've realized that *you* are the coworker." Calvin stepped to the kettle casually, in no particular hurry to silence it. He grabbed a mug from the shelf and set it on the counter. He only grabbed one.

"I'm sorry Calvin, I'm so, so sorry..."

"I don't think you understand, Myles."

"I'm sorry, I'm sorry...I got an invitation, I got excited, I never even considered—"

"You didn't give a damn *thought* about my life!" Calvin screamed.

"Calvin please! Don't go on like this!"

"You don't understand."

"Please forgive me, Calvin, I didn't know—"

"I am going to kill you, Myles."

The statement was said quietly, but with such force. It utterly silenced the entire room. A bead of sweat trickled down Myles's forehead—more followed in profuse excretion.

"Calvin..."

"I am going to kill you, Myles," he repeated. Then he withdrew the beautiful orb from his jacket.

The orb shone with *power*, with *force!* It was a lustrous red beauty, red as the scarlet blood on Calvin's hands, red as the harrowing ferocity in Calvin's eyes! The glass globe vibrated with alien intensity; it was fueled by hatred alone, hatred which *seared* like the summer Venus sun! Base anger—through this sphere of power—had been refined into pure energy.

The glass globe shuddered with erratic discharges of electromagnetic radiation. The kitchen light issued a loud report and, faltering, plunged the room in deep crimson. The entire house was filled with the domineering luster of the seductive sphere in Calvin's bloody hands.

"Calvin! You're not yourself!"

Calvin poured the shimmering scarlet liquid from the globe into the solitary mug on the counter. He placed the mug carefully in front of Myles, and looked at him in the dim twilight of the sphere.

"Drink. And die."

"Calvin, please! Why are you doing this!"

"Drink, Myles, drink!"

"Oh God please! Don't make me—"

"Drink, goddammit!"

Myles was sobbing; he had been forced to this horrific fate. He could consider no escape—Calvin's psychological terror saw to that. There was no alternative!

"Calvin—"

Calvin grabbed Myles' throat. Myles felt a warm, thick liquid stick to his skin. He writhed in Calvin's grasp. The mug came closer! Myles did not know what to do. In helpless obedience, his mouth broke free from his mind's influence. It opened...

The bright red fluid cascaded down his throat.

Myles felt the bodily deterioration begin. He felt a rapid loss of sensitivity. Sightless, soundless, tasteless, odorless—everything gone. As his mind descended into oblivion, he realized he no longer felt terror nor sorrow nor scorn.

He only felt forgiveness. Though his muscles would never express a message again, he had already forgiven Calvin...

II

Calvin choked on a sob. His hand fell away from Myles' still warm neck. His body rolled to the floor, quivering. His body convulsed uncontrollably. Now freed from the murderous influence of the glass globe, he saw what he had done.

"Myles!" Calvin screamed.

He had allowed himself to become the very corruption he swore to destroy. Calvin had descended into the very murderer he had sought and chased. He had inherited the qualities, the intentions—the hatred. The blurred line had been erased. There was no longer any distinction between them.

Calvin, exhausted, dropped all consideration of running away. He would stay here. He would accept judgement when it came in the morning, now less than twelve hours away...

Sixteen

"It is finished."

"The Project...is complete?"

"A phase of it, yes. Everything happened as I expected. Mr. Barker has become our murderer. And for this, he shall be prosecuted duly."

"Comatose..."

"Comatose is completely under our jurisdiction. I daresay it has been so for some time now."

"I am...slightly concerned, sir. Won't news of Comatose reach the great cities? Won't they sweep in here with their jet planes and their war machines aloft in the clouds?"

"You misunderstand the turmoil of the outside world, Demetria. The governments control nothing. They claim to run their advanced societies with precision and efficiency, but their skies are tumultuous with war. They too misunderstand—they misunderstand the problem of the world."

"Which is?"

"People. Human beings are the problem, and until there are less of them, the world will never know peace."

"Isn't it strange, though? The Project is finally complete!"

"Not remotely. Now that we know that it has succeeded within the bounds of Comatose, we must put it to use. Construction on the superseding satellite campus in Anesthesia will be finished within the next two years, fully equipped with everything necessary to serve as a world capital when the time comes."

"And the world will know peace."

"Long it has waited, Ms. McPherson. Long indeed."
"One last question, sir. Will you tell him?"
"Calvin? I shall. He regarded me as an enemy—but I always admired him, above all of the members of Paragon."
"Even Melissa?"
"Calvin had something over Melissa—a humble demeanor and a level-headed composure. And that is what distresses me so greatly: to see such an incorruptible figure corroded by greed, by hatred, by despair! Why do we fail, Demetria? Why does the world not forgive us our failures?"
"I haven't the answers, sir."
"Nobody does."

I.

MR. JARVIS MCCAIN WOKE FROM HIS UNEASY SLUMBER. FROM THE BED which denied him profitable sleep, he sat up and listened to the sounds of the night. He heard the crickets, and the beasts of twilight and all their music. But there were other sounds, sounds that he did not recognize—or at least associate with midnight noises. They were distant roars, the sigh of objects moving at incredible speeds through the dark.

"Cars..." he murmured.

Jarvis opened his mouth and allowed the distant noise to fill his body. He slowly untangled himself from the twisted sheets of sleeplessness and set his aching feet on cold hardwood. He entered the wide atrium of his home. The lights, sensing his presence, activated to their dim midnight presets.

In a moment he had the television up and running. Rapidly he flipped through the meaningless sitcoms and porn musicals and sudden-death gameshows. He came to the region of news broadcast stations and still could not find what he was searching for.

Finally, on an obscure channel of questionable repute, he found a self-proclaimed station proclaiming the news:

MASSIVE EMIGRATION OF CARS OUTTA NOWHERE!
STAY TUNED WHEN WE RETURN!

Jarvis forced himself to remain on the channel as the advertisements fluttered past like torrents of colorful birds, as men and women so glamorous they were no longer beautiful filled the screen to the brim with wickedness. Jarvis turned his eyes from the television in disgust—this was all people desired now. What rational media outlet would linger upon the truth when the money lies in sensationalism?

A circus came to his mind—that was the world of information now. Make them laugh! Make them smile! Make them feel safe and secure in their conviction that things will never change, direct their money to recipients who need it least and their attention where it makes no difference! Keep them drunk and high and content beyond their wildest dreams, but for the sake of the show, dammit, don't give them *truth!*

Truth sobers, truth saddens, truth turns away the eager customer and shames him! There is no circus without a carefree audience—keep the entertainment up! *This* circus is here to stay.

An anchor, at last, appeared on the screen. He wore a wide smile that broadcasted a sense of faux surety to the audience.

"A long stream of vehicles has been coming down from the uninhabited countryside in a mass exodus! The vehicles' origins? We haven't the faintest. What's that?"

The man paused and frowned as an attendant brought him a piece of paper with more information.

"Ah! Just in, folks. Our team just interviewed some of the drivers, and it sounds like they're coming from a village called...er, I'm sorry, Commatown. Haha!" The anchor's smile reappeared. "Looks like no one wants to *come* to Commatown!"

Jarvis turned off the television.

He walked to the dark windows and stared out at the sky. The clouds were stained in deep crimson from the long trails of the jetfighters. Never had he found any explanation of their presence on those news stations. Always shrouded in mystery, as all truths were.

He paused to think about Melissa. And then he thought about Calvin, whom he had always regarded as a son. He thought of all the pent-up anger within the boy. Jarvis realized, with an unexpected concern, the loneliness that separated Calvin from others.

In his stomach Jarvis felt a sudden icy cold, like the steel knife of an unseen emotion. But he could not explain why...

He looked out the window again and contemplated the dark future of the world.

II

THE PHANTOMS FELL IN BEHIND EACH OTHER AS THE SNOW RESUMED that morning. At times becoming one with the snow, the vehicles rolled along the street, their manner contemptuous towards the desolate city.

Three of the phantoms broke off from the stream before reaching the Cross. They were of a different commission, a task that would operate in secrecy while others addressed the people that remained, the people that ignored even the paralyzing fear that surrounded them day after day.

The phantoms continued until reaching a negligible side-street known as Calle del Durmiente. Turning onto this road, only the crunching of snow underfoot penetrated the quilt of quietude that had woven itself around the city.

The cars reached, at last, the final house on the street. Here, they would arrest and apprehend the Bane of Comatose, the murderer, the gloved hand of white velvet, the dealer of sleep and thief of sanity.

The members disembarked—these were the members of the Enforcement Unit, the most elite of peacekeepers, the most qualified enactors of the law.

Dressed in cream-colored Italian suits with neither padding nor weapon, equipped with neither battering ram nor megaphone, the Enforcement Unit assembled themselves before the door. Their leader removed an unassuming metal ring from his finger—a modest implement with ten thousand keys programmed into its memory.

With a deft movement the ring was brought parallel with the lock. Upon spoken word, the ring released a cloud of nano-matter at the lock. A temporary key assembled itself, opened the door, and fizzled into vapor as its constituent parts returned to the leader's ring.

The Enforcement Unit entered the living room softly. Finding it empty, they proceeded to the kitchen. There, by the table, two men slept. But only one would wake again.

The peacekeepers crouched by the man in the chair. They observed him in unison, shook their heads in mock pity, and then glanced at the second man on the floor. The men nodded, and softly shook him awake.

When the man began to stir, the Enforcement Unit patiently waited until he reacted to their interrogative glance.

"Sir? Are you Calvin Barker?" the leader asked.

The man looked directly into their faces and allowed his mouth to open in a silent scream of despair. He coughed and rasped, and looked as if he was unable to produce coherent speech.

The men waited patiently.

Finally, the response came: "Not anymore."

Their reply was laced with feigned compassion. "Mr. Barker, we are, regrettably, here to arrest you. We have a court order signed by The Municipal Chancellor."

"To hell with your Municipal Chancellor."

"Now, now, we can't have that. Are you able to stand, sir?"

"Who are you?"

"We are the eye of the storm. We are the intercessors between you and the furious world. We mean no offense, Mr. Barker, but you have committed a terrible crime. It would be an injustice to see it go unpunished, sir. Such things simply must be done."

"I can stand," Calvin growled. He rose steadily, aided by two other members of the Enforcement Unit. Another member strode to the counter, where sat the glass globe, drained of all that had made it valuable. This man said to his superior: "Commander? What shall we do with this?"

"The poison? Destroy it as soon as you can, Lieutenant. It's caused enough damage already."

Calvin blinked, and looked at the commander with a confused face.

"Don't fear, Mr. Barker," the commander said. "The Municipal Chancellor has prepared an audience with you, and he has more answers than I do. Now, if you'll come along, sir."

Calvin began to move, but before he left the house he glanced back at the first man, the man who would never wake again. He glanced at Myles.

"What will you do with him?" Calvin murmured, a voice filled with sorrow and deep regret.

"I cannot understand why that would concern you, sir," the commander answered. There was no trace of scorn in those words, but it marked a slight lapse in the man's cordiality. He turned to his lieutenant. "Have the body delivered to the hospital."

The commander led Calvin to the waiting phantoms. The back door was opened for him. He stepped into the cream leather-padded interior with neither thought of the present nor care for the future. He had severed the final ties that connected him with humanity. Now freed from those marionette strings, he did not know what he was. Freedom was falsehood—something he finally understood. Once a man had exercised his freedom to the fullest extent possible, he was no longer a man at all. He was a nobody, trapped and imprisoned outside of everything that he wanted to become once more. Estranged by freedom.

The commander was driving them away from the cursed residence. He was talking. "I really want to thank you, Mr. Barker. Your cooperation was not entirely anticipated."

"Will that help me at all? Give me any leverage when the sentence arrives?"

The man, for the first time, laughed at him. "If cooperation could redeem murder, Mr. Barker, what a terrible world we would be living in."

III

FROM THE BACK SEAT OF THE OBSIDIAN PANTHER, MR. MORGAN Powers stared out thoughtfully. He considered; he contemplated; he wondered. He considered the future; he considered what it had in store for the people of the world. He contemplated the past; he contemplated how it had finally yielded the events necessary for dramatic change.

And he wondered. He wondered about Calvin Barker.

Powers knew what had to be done. There was no doubt about this. He felt as an artist might, forced by poverty to live on the streets, with no choice but to sell his paintings or destroy them. He wondered, and contemplated, and considered. Calvin, though once the owner of an unparalleled mind, was no longer sane. Powers would do what he must.

With every facet of the law to back him up, he still felt hesitant to fulfill his duty. It would be like punishing a child for crime it neither understood nor recognized. So, Powers formulated his plan: he would take Calvin aside, teach him the truth, and then...

He need not plan that far. He knew what would be done.

Presently, the panther reached the Cross. Powers disembarked and strode towards the dais from where he made his speeches. He glanced up at the glass statue being assembled in the center of the park.

He looked at his coworkers, the various chairmen and chairwomen of the Academy's leading teams. They smiled at him with pride. He looked at the assemblage of citizens. Despite multiple tallies, he could only bring the count to fifteen. Fifteen citizens, who had neither fled nor succumbed to Comatose. Fifteen.

Then he gingerly lifted a hand to the sky, before all of those gathered before the dais. And he began to tell them a story. He began to tell them of the victory of the Academy's team. He began to tell them of the long awaited freedom—the freedom from fear and death and hatred.

He began to tell them of the story of Calvin Barker, a detective turned murderer, finally apprehended and brought to justice...

IV

From the glass elevator, Calvin looked upon the desolate city of Comatose. Without seeing, he saw the destruction. Without hearing, he heard the laments of anguish. For though Comatose had not changed in appearance, it was no longer a city. And though the woeful cries had been silenced, he heard the echoes, over and over again, a throb of harrowing, horrifying accusation: *Calvin please! Don't go on like this!*

He glanced down at his hands, their scars an incriminating memory of what he had done. Neither chains nor strong arms restrained him. The Academy was not afraid of Calvin Barker. A pair of campus security officers stood on either side, simply to ensure he reached his final destination.

Only a promise kept him there, a promise made by Morgan Powers, a promise to reveal everything that had happened and why it had. The desire to understand the truth was far more confining than any pair of handcuffs.

The elevator stopped. Here, in Powers' office—like Room 101—they would break him. Here, at the top of the world, Calvin would know death at last.

The guards did not exit the elevator. They gestured toward the office at the end of the antechamber, and Calvin knew what happened next. He took a step into the carpeted, mahogany-paneled room, and then he took another. The elevator closed.

"Forward, then," Calvin whispered. To this point he had feigned the absence of fear—but he was only human. No power beneath the sun could wipe away the strength of shame; only punishment would suffice. And there, in that dreaded room, he would meet it.

Calvin felt weightless. In his mind, he set the gilded doors adrift with the slightest touch. He was in the massive office now.

Before him stood Morgan Powers, Executive Chairman, God of Deception, Municipal Chancellor of The World.

"Mr. Barker."

Calvin understood, at last, the fear! He understood the absolute terror he ought to have felt before this man, this majestic display of supremacy. The man, dressed in a long black tailcoat and vest above a stiff-collared crimson shirt to contrast, was sharp as a deadly sword and inflexible as a diamond. No higher authority beneath the heavens existed—the judgement that followed would be second to God's alone.

"Sit down, Calvin."

A chair was brought forth. Calvin sat.

The enemy likewise seated himself at his odious desk. Behind the man, visible through multi-faceted squares of glass, lay the entire world, placed there like an afterthought, a backdrop, a meaningless expression of authority.

"Consider the World, Calvin Barker!" Powers began. "Consider your significance, my significance, the significance of all the people who have ever lived and died on the surface of our planet. Close your eyes; consider all of them, Calvin."

Calvin closed his eyes, considering the people of the world.

Powers continued. "Now people are very diverse and unique, but they share similarities. You have your genders and your skin colors and your creeds and religions and political schools of thought, insignificant in one respect: they do not truly classify a human being. There is, in fact, only one thing that truly classifies a human being, Calvin. Do you know it?"

Calvin did not understand how—but he *did* know the answer. It struck him with grief—because it was true of him especially. When he spoke, his voice was thick and slurred:

"Evil."

"Impressive, Calvin. No matter what they say—the peacemakers, the humanitarians, the champions of free will and democracy—mankind is evil. Evil is often dramatized—truly, the word represents an action done to achieve one's own purposes in conscious violation of another's. Those who perpetrate capital evils know to manipulate the ignorance present in mankind's culture—

ignorance which has grown exponentially across these dark years. Evil feeds on ignorance, even innocence! The opposite of ignorance is vigilance, Mr. Barker."

Calvin looked at Powers, waiting for the loose ends to converge.

"To solve the world's problems has always been a goal of the philanthropist. But we now are faced with solving the World Problem—evil itself. We are given two ways, Calvin, two options. One is to eradicate evil directly—the flawed method used time and time again throughout the years! The second," Powers smiled, "is more unique. Think about it, Calvin! Instead of extinguishing the fire, we extinguish the fuel! Promote vigilance—by eradicating ignorance."

Calvin looked at Powers in confusion. This was making sense, but it seemed to glorify the wrong side...

"Before Comatose, before the city even began to prosper, there was the Academy," Powers continued. "We model ourselves after the Athenians: the ancient Academy of Plato, the first institution of its kind amidst an ignorant, uneducated world.

"You see, *our* Academy is much the same. We are something new in a world of ancient assumptions. At our core, there stands a simple, double-pronged concept known as The Project. Every member of the Academy knew how grand, how vast and majestic The Project would be—but how delicate, how dangerous and risky as well. We begin with a test community, a small, unassuming village full of unassuming people. We drain the ignorance out while maintaining the pressure! Equilibrium maintained, but equilibrium of a different material entirely! Instead of a healthy balance of good and evil, we have a healthy balance of good and good!"

Calvin finally spoke up. "You're talking about eradicating ignorance—ignorance prevalent in...people?"

Powers looked down at Calvin firmly.

"Yes, Calvin. I might as well say it bluntly: We are the murderer."

Calvin stared at the man, his enemy revealed at last. But, bound to the promise of truth, he did not move.

"The world is filled with confused people, Calvin. People who think they know what they want, people who will go out of their way to *ensure* that they get what they want! Without a thought or care towards the goals of the world, people waste their lives on themselves instead of using them towards the benefit of others! People who do such things are trivial, useless. So trivial, in fact, that the philosophies constituting The Project have no objection in eliminating such parasites."

Calvin exploded. "Who killed those people? Who killed Miss Brady? Who killed Kaufmann? Who killed the councilors and the drunkards and the 'insignificant' people? Who killed Melissa?!" He was standing, towering over his still seated enemy.

Powers regarded him coldly. "Who killed Myles?"

Calvin stumbled backward into his chair as though he'd been shot. The reminder was clear—could he assume the place of the judge while blood yet stained his hands?

"Every 'murder,' as you call it, was done with intention," Powers continued. "The city of Comatose, absent of all wrongdoers, is now safer than ever before!"

Calvin retorted. "Of course the city is absent of wrongdoers! You yourself told me that every damned human being is a *wrongdoer!* Where are your people, Powers? You have no citizens left!"

Powers blinked. "People themselves are the problem. When we at last diminish the human race to a manageable quantity—"

"Then you will truly have nothing left! Your variables have all dropped out! Zero equals Zero! It's meaningless, everything meaningless!"

Powers finally stood. He reached into his desk as if to assure himself that a certain object was there. Then, to Calvin: "It seems that our conversation concerning society has...expired. The time has come, my friend."

"You haven't told me how you killed them all."

From the desk Powers extracted an indescribable instrument of immeasurable complexity and shape and placed it before the other's eyes. Calvin, from his chair, examined it until he became sick with confusion.

"You need not study it until I turn it on. It is called a Sensory Overload Machine. It does not penetrate the skin and therefore leaves no trace of its usage. The machine first will confuse you. It will present you will so many feelings and sights and sounds that your body will be unable to process it all. In a matter of seconds, all of the brain cells that detect and handle information will be overwhelmed—dead. And after your mind recovers from the initial 'knock-out', the remainder of your brain will have no way to prove that you still exist. You will continue on, a sightless, soundless, tasteless, odorless, unfeeling ghost, living and living and *living* until you will yourself to die from self-loathing. A true, absolutely efficient tool of murder."

Calvin shuddered; Calvin trembled. In a matter of minutes he would be subjected to this torture.

"There is no *one* murderer, Calvin—it is the collective opinion of those united for the greater good. The man or woman who physically performs the killing is acting under the influence of us all. It is a burden that we bear jointly. But you...you have killed for your own gain. And it will not be tolerated in the society to come. We, the united collective, the Academy, condemn you to die by this method, in accordance with your crimes."

The security men had returned unnoticed. Calvin tried to stand, to rise, to run!—but their hands clamped around him like anchors and his body strained to no avail. Powers, like a sacrificial priest, held aloft the golden instrument.

"Powers, you're insane! Killing everyone won't save the world, it will end it! There is no way to achieve your goal!"

The man spoke no more. He touched the instrument lightly, and death began.

The myriad of golden needles grew longer and began to quiver. A low-pitched sound began, then a slightly higher sound, and another. Soon the machine would play every note of every octave of every scale at the exact same time, in horrible, earsplitting dissonance. From the golden needles sprouted minuscule golden threads. Calvin, entranced, was held motionless by forces unknown. The machine continued to sing, the threads wrapped around his arms, the needles quivered.

And then the machine was a brilliant sphere of light, millions upon millions of colors at the same time, colors never seen before, impossible colors not found on the electromagnetic spectrum! But Calvin's brain could process them all, during this final bid for life. His brain processed the sound and the sights and the quivering of the threads and the sounds and the sights and the quivering and the sounds and the sights...

Finally, with a desperate scream, his dying mind hovering between earth and the realms beyond, he grasped a critical secret from eternity and spewed it into the mortal world:

"Love! The answer is love!"

Powers did not have time to react when the machine exploded. The impact knocked him to the floor and left a thick, burning smell in the office. Silence consumed all. For a precious few moments, everything was still.

Finally, trembling, Powers stood and looked at Calvin Barker, who sat lifeless in the chair. The security men were sprawled upon the floor, too close to the explosion and severely wounded.

But Powers rushed instead to Calvin's arm. He delicately placed his quivering fingers over the artery. He found no pulse. Calvin was dead, truly dead!

Calvin had been set free.

A Postmortem

The Academy
503 Avenue Grande
Comatose Municipality
Global Cooperation Initiative

From the desk of Morgan Powers;
Executive Chairman of the Academy,
Municipal Chancellor of the City of Comatose,

A Postmortem,
concerning the success of The Comatose Project:

I have always found, from early on, a great
fascination for human nature. I have studied it
immensely, not from a controlled lab with
sensitive instruments—I have studied it as one who
is among it. And there I have set the chief
distinction between myself and the learned
scholars who call themselves philosophers,
psychologists, professors. I have studied the
world and its people—not by way of assumption, but
by way of *gambling*. I do not say of the common
man: "He may have done this out of love, or
desire, or pride, but we do not know for certain."
Surely, this phrase is the all-inclusive
embodiment of accuracy—but it is too general to be
accurate in the slightest. It is rather like
attempting to catch a goldfish with a net made for
salmon: Certainly you will enclose the creature in
the net, but the goldfish—the true meaning—will
escape through the gaps.
 I consider it nothing short of a gift, my
ability to discern the human psyche. After years
of honing my gambling technique, I have found that
not once have I ever made a mistake in guessing

why a certain man or woman behaved a certain way. It was, with this skill in mind, that I devised the Comatose Project.

The title itself was not such, when I first conceived it. For, as the reader may have guessed by this time, I did not know *where* my idea would work. I also knew that it would not have worked some seventy years earlier. In those days, perhaps stemming from the years following 2000, the world became obsessed with popular media. Not *important* media, but popular. The world, given ten more years, found itself tired of the horrid news. And her media, sensing the discomfort, began showing only the pieces that the people wanted to see.

Thus began a trend of ignorance. Thus began a rapid disintegration of human diversity. With less curiosity, the human mind became easier to understand, and easier to manipulate. I watched the course of history. In less than a century, the world was ready for a change. The entire system was a strong oak with feeble roots. With a mere gesture, I found a way to supplant it.

I did not start right away. I needed a test society, and this was found in the secluded, ignorant town of Comatose. I set up our establishment quite quickly, and built up a reputation of imperial standard. Then, I began The Project. The goal? To topple the town's ruling body without open war—and to have a better system ready to replace the old.

A volatile element of fear became essential, and this I found in the Sensory Overload Machine. It left virtually no trace of its usage save for an impossibly negligible caution: With the correct, expensive instruments, a recording of extremely high brain activity could be yielded in the few minutes directly following the permanent coma. This, however, would leave only speculation as to what had caused the brain death, not who. And so The Murderer, as we coined it, remained unseen. Meanwhile, a path to victory was under construction, detailing the necessary victims and the chronological sequence of their "execution." This was essential.

We also had to involve an organization that could control what was discovered. Having already established a lasting reputation, the Academy built a strong, reputable team of detectives who would work for the city but were answerable to myself alone. This team of detectives superseded the ignorant police force because of our supposed diligence. Now, with my hand controlling not only how the deaths occurred but also how they were investigated, I felt a strong assurance in my ability to pull off the perfect *coup d'état*.

The Project encountered but one small dilemma which impeded the speed at which it moved— I had neither the trust nor the ignorance of the Mayor, Mr. Samuel Kaufmann. Under his direction, a new opponent was created: Paragon Private Investigations. A game of chess ensued. The strict rules of play, the sequence, the order of death— these were set aside, to be designated as mere "guidelines." Finally, I had the chance to put my own intellect to the test, against hundreds upon thousands of ever-changing variables.

The death of Melissa McCain was one of my more tormented moments in the game. For she was the Queen piece, the strongest—and therefore the most loftily paraded. I arranged for the bait, using the phone from my own desk to lure her to the Cross. On the rooftops above I had stationed, to my great annoyance, a ruthless mercenary with a rocket. (This man was killed, by means of Sensory Overload Machine, not ten seconds following his crime.) Then the bomb exploded, and I assumed that Melissa had perished most unduly. I met great delight, therefore, in the discovery of her continued existence. Having weakened her vigilance by great measures, I found grim satisfaction in personally delivering the final blow.

I find it necessary to refute the reader's cry of disgust—I still regret this single deed. The fortunes of Comatose rose and fell, but my mind still lingered on what I had done. I consecrated the death toward the future of the world, and swore that no person would ever truly *leave* the world to reach that future. The Sensory Overload Machine did not cause death, but a permanent unconsciousness. I championed this over the bloody means of murder.

The case of Myles Goodrich and Calvin Barker was most interesting. I had not even begun to predict that there was anything unstable in Calvin's nature—but following Melissa's death, I began to reassess him. I tempted him with the "poison," a chemical substitute for the Sensory Overload Machine. Doctor Vescovi and his coworkers crafted it as well as they could, but I am not entirely certain that the effects are the same...or even permanent, for that matter. I gave Calvin the poison with feigned reluctance and offered Myles lofty titles so as to induce jealousy and hate within Calvin. The exact way Myles perished remains unknown to me—but as a scholar of human nature, I would have sacrificed much in order to witness it!

Calvin's own death was educational, but also fitting. I realized, under the pressure of death and hatred, that Calvin was no longer the controlled man that I knew him to be. It has prompted a study which I shall continue in the following years. Though distracted with arranging a grand insurrection against the Global Cooperation Initiative, I still intend to pursue a new field: The study of inherent evil. And because it seems to me that no man can study his own disease, I must create a machine that can do so for us. It will prompt a most exciting discovery.

Until then, I daresay that the future remains promising.

(Signed) Morgan Powers